CW00853482

PASSPORT TO LOVE

A story of Resilience, Redemption and a Quest for Love

Cécile Rischmann

AMAZON LLC

To Akash,
With Love,
Rischmann

Copyright © 2024 Cécile Rischmann

All rights reserved

The characters and events portrayed in this book are fictitious. Any similarity to real persons, living or dead, is coincidental and not intended by the author.

No part of this book may be reproduced, or stored in a retrieval system, or transmitted in any form or by any means, electronic, mechanical, photocopying, recording, or otherwise, without express written permission of the publisher.

ASIN: B0D2ZY6CQQ
ISBN: 9798324349660

Cover design by: Art Painter
Library of Congress Control Number: 2018675309
Printed in the United States of America

To my beloved family, especially my husband, whose unwavering love and support have guided me through every twist and turn of this journey. To my cherished friends, your encouragement and belief in me have fueled my determination to see this project through. And to my well-wishers, thank you for standing by me and believing in the power of my words. This book is dedicated to each one of you.

CHAPTER ONE

Bureau, Rescue Operations, Gurgaon, India.

The telephone shrilled as Sid Chevalier strode into his office. He picked up the receiver on the fourth ring when he couldn't spot his efficient receptionist, Anna, at her desk, nor his faithful right-hand man, Roy, at his. The bureau seemed too peaceful for a Monday morning, he thought, peeping into his assistant Rebecca's cabin and finding it empty, too.

Where was everyone? He didn't pay them to sleep!

"Sid Chevalier," he said as he dropped into a vacant chair near the front desk. A woman's heart-wrenching sobs erupted from the other end of the receiver. His jaw clenched, and his hands balled into fists. She sounded like she had reached the end of her control, and it took Sid back in time to when he was a helpless toddler watching his father beat up his mother. Sid pushed his memories aside and inhaled deeply, reminding himself that he had come a long way from then.

"I'm sorry," she sniffled. "I'm Jasmine Chari."

"Where are you, Mrs Chari?" He picked up a pen, opened a fresh page, and noted the details. His vision blurred as he stared out of the window, oblivious to the beautiful glass bureau occupying most of the cabin. The thick plantation beyond the glass panes soared towards the sky, adding to the aesthetic beauty of the building. The wide MG Road stretched before him, painted with a fluid stream of morning traffic.

He angrily scribbled 'Residential Towers, Gurgaon' on the sheet, cursing his father and men like him who derived pleasure

1

from harming defenceless women. The woman wasn't poor if she stayed in that place, he thought. *But not necessarily happy*, a little voice insisted. "Do you have children, Mrs Chari?"

The question triggered another bout of sobbing from Mrs Chari. Sid looked around him helplessly, wishing he had some assistance on this call. Anna was trained to deal with the callers, while Sid, Roy, and Rebecca handled the abusers.

The footsteps in the outer corridor signalled the arrival of Roy, his colleague and a police officer. About time! The man with salt-and-pepper hair was in his early sixties. He shed his shapeless suede jacket in the closet. He hung his cap beside it, revealing khaki trousers and a crisp white shirt, the only evidence that he was once a police officer who had earned his stripes but lost his family. Now retired, Roy worked day and night tirelessly, dedicated to bringing criminals to justice and keeping the streets safe.

Roy eased himself onto the chair, and it winced under his weight. He powered on his desktop, and the screen came to life, revealing a map that pinpointed the caller's location. He minimised the map and opened another program that coughed vital information about Mrs Chari. He printed the relevant details and compiled the data into a comprehensive file.

"Two. Reshmi is eleven, and Mira is five," Mrs Chari said.

Minors! This is going to be complicated. Their bureau was already facing backlash for their efforts to help women restart their lives independently, leaving their abusive partners behind. The traditional folks who believed in the sanctity of marriage viewed Rescue Operations as breaking up marriages by providing an exit for women seeking a way out.

"You need to be strong, Mrs Chari. We're going to get you out," Sid said.

From the doorway, the scent of J'Adore wafted into the room, announcing the arrival of Rebecca Crawford, his efficient investigator and trained black belt. Rebecca, affectionately called Becka. In her late twenties, Rebecca could draw attention effortlessly with her azure eyes, waist-length blond hair, and voluptuous curves.

Sid's irritation grew as he watched Roy, who had been diligently focusing on the Chari file, suddenly shift his attention and dramatically exhale between his parted lips. For an intelligent man, Roy was acting incredibly silly. As for Rebecca, she had a provocative smile on her face, but as soon as she noticed Sid looking in their direction, she said something under her breath, and sat down. Roy turned back to his screen.

Anna tiptoed to her desk, running late as usual. However, she froze midway when she saw Sid sitting nearby. Her steps faltered, and she quickly scurried to the board, stammering a greeting with the look of a whipped puppy.

What a team they made!

"I'll be there in twenty minutes, Mrs Chari. Keep the doors unlocked. No chauffeurs or maids around. Hide in the washroom with your children. I'll deal with the security." He waited for Mrs Chari to disconnect and then replaced the receiver.

The office started to breathe as the team sprang into action. Printers whirred, phones shrilled, and the air conditioners hummed. Rebecca had joined Roy; their heads were close together as they pooled their expertise. Anna was in her element at the board, listening attentively to callers and providing soothing assistance. Sid felt fortunate to have such a dedicated team by his side. Their collective efforts had propelled Rescue Operations to become one of the top ten rescue bureaus in India.

As Sid paced back and forth in his office, he couldn't shake off the nagging feeling that he needed to handle the case himself. Roy and Rebecca were indeed capable officers who had proven their efficiency in handling previous cases for Rescue Operations. However, Sid felt a strong personal connection to the case this time.

"Shall we proceed, boss?" Roy asked.

Sid halted his pacing, head and shoulders above Roy. The physical activity helped to calm his mind, but his heart thudded with fear—fear of what would happen to Mrs Chari if her husband came to know that she had called for rescue.

"Not this time, Roy." Sid massaged the back of his neck as the muscles started to cramp. At least Mrs Chari had called for assistance. It was a good sign. He wished his mother had done the same all those years ago. His jaw clenched with suppressed emotion. A day didn't pass by without him thinking of his mother. His whole life revolved around finding her again—if she was alive. This entire business of rescuing women began only because of his mother. Sid had left a well-paid job in France and his adopted parents and had come to his country of origin (India) to find his mother.

"I need to do this myself, Roy." Her painful cries still echoed in his mind as his father assaulted her night after night—sometimes, during the day, too. Sid was only three years old then and had watched helplessly.

His hands trembled as he combed his fingers through his thick, dark hair, looking at the photo frame hanging on the wall in his office. It was the only snapshot he had of his mother. She was wearing a cotton sari, her long, black hair freshly washed and adorned with jasmine flowers. In her arms, she carried a bundle clutched to her chest... and that bundle was Sid.

Yes, he was doing it for his mother, the only woman he loved.

Rebecca's plucked brows arched. "You need assistance, boss. You'll be outnumbered. Mrs Chari's husband is a top-notch businessman with connections..."

Sid nodded, acknowledging Rebecca's concern. He knew Mrs Chari's husband could be a formidable opponent with his wealth, power, and connections. However, Sid was undeterred.

He had faced challenges in his career and learned to navigate difficult situations with his experience and skills.

"Boss," Rebecca's expression softened, "it's time you let old wounds heal. You couldn't do anything for your mother then... you were three years old! I know you want to make it up to your mother, but this case is complicated and involves a celebrity couple."

Roy nodded, agreeing with Rebecca. "I don't think we should take on this case, boss. The law will be on Sunil's side as he is Indian. Mrs Chari and her children are French citizens with OCI (Overseas Citizen of India)," he said. "Let's refer Mrs Chari to another bureau."

Sid looked at his mother's picture. *What do you say, Amma? Should I save Mrs Chari?*

Her jet-black eyes seemed to pierce him. *Of course, you must save her, Siddhu. You promised her.*

Rebecca's modulated voice interrupted the silent communication. "Sunil Chari reins the stock market..."

Roy hurried to her side, trying to lighten the situation. "Maybe Becka can come with you, boss. She can divert your opponent while you play the hero."

Pale, unsmiling blue eyes fastened on Roy, the earlier camaraderie seeming to have vanished. "I didn't become a black belt to distract people, Roy. The next time you say something like that, I'll knock you down," Rebecca said in soft, menacing tones.

Sid shot Roy an irritated glance. Couldn't he be serious for once? "She's right, Roy. You owe Becka an apology. I'll wait for the update, Becka." He collected his vest from the closet, shoved his arms into the sleeves, and sheathed his well-toned abs. He could feel Becka's blue stare riding up his sculpted body in a slow, appreciative way that made Sid wish he was wearing a sack.

If only Becka weren't such a good investigator, he'd have sacked her on the grounds of sexual harassment, he thought with a weary sigh. Tucking his pistol in his belt (the perks of being in the gendarmerie.) But, of course, he had to comply with the local laws and regulations in obtaining a permit to work under the special arrangements between the law enforcement agencies of their countries. He strode out, wishing Roy, Becka, and Anna a good day.

*

The silver Porsche growled to life under Sid's expert hands, and he let her run unleashed, having a valid reason: Jasmine Chari. His hands tightened on the steering wheel, willing the tension to leave his body. The roaring beast devoured the twenty-minute drive from his office and glided to a halt at the check post, and he could feel the piercing curiosity in the eyes of the uniformed officers.

Sid grinned. No one would guess who he was. Rebecca had given him some sound instructions. *Wear your cap low over your head; sunglasses should cover most of your face. Give the impression of a young gigolo on call.*

"Thank you, Becka," he mumbled under his breath as they flagged him in. His eyes shone with humour as he remembered Becka at their first meeting. It had been at a party held by the sponsors on the eve of the International Black Belt Tournament. Sid had made the mistake of laughing when Becka stated that she could take him on. He later realised she was a dangerous opponent. What a fight it had been! Of course, Sid had won in the end, but she had given him a tough run, and his respect had mounted.

His foot pressed on the accelerator, and the beast zoomed down the palm-tree pathway and multi-coloured flowers bordering the tracks that ran uphill towards the eight-story luxurious building. Vast landscaped lawns stretched out, adorned with amenities designed for indulgence and leisure. The tennis and basketball courts promised hours of friendly competition and skilful play. A cosy clubhouse stood as a haven for relaxation and socialisation while a conveniently located supermarket catered to every need. Clusters of lush plants and shrubs offered a serene sanctuary, creating a sense of tranquillity. And at the heart of it all, an Olympic-size pool shimmered invitingly.

High-resolution cameras were set up strategically everywhere.

His gaze riveted on the glass tower as he slid out of his low-slung car (a gift to himself for all the years of hard work). The gold and cream interiors of the building were extravagant but toned down by the simple design. The green marble flooring shone under LED bulb strips fixed to the false ceiling. Illuminated potted plants adorned the place, softening the ambience and giving it a homely feel.

As Sid strode towards the iron grill gates, he nodded at the security guard stationed there, a burly figure whose stern expression hinted at a strict adherence to duty. The guard's features bore the unmistakable air of someone more comfortable conversing in Hindi. As Sid swiped his card operating on a caller ID facility, he punched in the apartment number, hoping Mrs Chari remembered the instructions.

"Sid Chevalier," he said into the receiver, hiding his impatience when a child answered. "Is your mom there?"

"Amma is sick," she said with a slight lisp.

Sid smiled despite himself, thinking of his nieces in France. He should invite them over for vacations. They would love India. His stepsister, Charlotte, had never resented Sid's presence and had always made him feel welcome in the family. He'd never forget how she taught him French and helped him integrate with their culture. She even enrolled him in martial arts when she saw him getting beaten up on several occasions.

"I'm Amma's friend," he said. From the corner of his eyes, he caught a glimpse of the guard's furrowed brow. He didn't relish the thought of asking him for assistance in case Little Miss Chari couldn't manage the task.

"Are you Superman?" she gushed, releasing the gates in an instant. "Amma said Superman is going to save us."

Sid felt an unfamiliar tightening in his chest, thinking of the helpless woman weaving tales to keep her children hopeful. He stepped inside the building, scanning the corridors as he strode. Ignoring the chrome and glass elevators and the service lifts, he ran up the stairway.

The Chari's condominium occupied the eighth floor, and the corridors boasted expansive wall-to-wall windows that welcomed the gentle embrace of sunlight. Potted plants decorated the *passage*, releasing pleasant scents that teased his senses. His gaze settled upon the solid triple-lock teak-wood door to Mrs Chari's residence, and a momentary wave of doubt made his shoulders sag. Had Mrs Chari remembered to leave the door unlocked as he had instructed her? Should he have to test his strength against that formidable barrier? He exhaled in relief as the door swung open.

The sweet perfume of jasmine flowers continued to engulf him as he advanced. On his left was the dining hall, with its sliding glass doors leading to balconies adorned with potted plants, their vibrant presence bringing life and colour to the room. On his right was the lounge, where a pristine white piano sat in the centre. Red silk drapes were drawn across the sunlit balcony, casting a reddish glow inside.

An ominous silence persisted inside the apartment, apart from the clawing and scraping of pigeons perched in the shadow of the window loft, their distinctive chirps somewhat noisy.

Sid felt his inner alarm chime as he was midway to the dining hall. He did a swift pirouette, his hand reaching for the reassuring touch of the cold metal of his pistol, holstered at his hip. At first, he saw nothing, but being over six feet tall, it was easy to overlook someone barely reaching his thighs.

Little Miss Mira, he assumed, as his eyes swept downwards. She was clasping a tattered teddy bear to her chest, her wide, dark eyes running up his long legs and trying to take in his towering form. He dropped on one knee before she got a crick in her neck.

"Superman here!" he said.

Dark, terrified eyes caught his. *Superman wasn't so tall,* she seemed to say. *He always came in costume. He didn't walk in; he climbed in through windows.*

"Where's your Superman dress?" she demanded in a shaky voice.

Sid controlled his smile, wishing he could scoop her in his arms and give her a reassuring hug. But in his profession, it didn't pay to be too affectionate as his actions could be misunderstood.

"I have it underneath," he whispered. "Where is your amma?"

The black head tipped forward, and she started to move the weight of her body alternately from the left foot to the right foot. Her grip loosened around her teddy bear, and it tumbled onto the soft Kashmiri carpet. Sid picked it up and gave it back to her, and she crushed it to her chest.

"Appa beat Amma again," she said. One hand pointed towards the master suite located down the dimly lit corridor. "Reshmi fights Appa, and Appa beats Reshmi. Mira cry." She looked at Sid as if she was expecting him to throw her appa out of the window.

What kind of environment was this for children? Beating his wife was bad enough, but to beat his children?

Better get the job done, Sid, and leave. The last thing you need right now is to get emotionally involved in the case.

A sudden movement in the darkened corridors snapped Sid to attention. Something... no, someone... was hurtling towards him with unexpected speed Before he could comprehend what was happening, a young girl with twin braids flying behind her leapt onto him, sending him stumbling backwards and colliding with the wall, making him momentarily lose his breath.

As he gathered his composure, he took in the courageous girl—undoubtedly Reshmi, imagining how she must have been honing her skills out of necessity. But enough was enough. Despite Reshmi's small size, the determined girl had managed to land two punches and deliver a kick. Sid caught hold of her wriggling form and lifted her into the air. He shook her lightly with a firm yet gentle grip, conveying a sense of authority and asserting his presence.

"Who are you?" Her chin jutted out, her hand inching towards the receiver fixed on the wall. "I'll give you five seconds before I call security."

Sid's heart tugged despite the undeserved punches he had received, thinking of Reshmi alone, battling with grown-up men to shield her mother and sister. His talkative and informative companion, Mira, had switched sides, hiding behind her sister and monitoring Sid from a distance.

Reshmi was breathing hard, and her determined expression made it clear that she meant what she said. Sid knew that the entire operation would be jeopardised if she called security. What's more, Mrs Chari would have to step in and rescue him! Enough of drama; he better get them out of there before the next member arrived.

"I'm looking for Mrs Chari."

Reshmi's eyes narrowed, and she suddenly grabbed a golf club from a bag lying unnoticed in a corner. Goodness! He could recruit her for Rescue Operations, Sid thought with a grim smile and jerked the weapon out of her hand while holding her gaze.

"I'm from the—police." He'd explain later about Rescue Operations. It appeared that Mrs Chari hadn't discussed her call apart from the Superman story, but again, she would have probably thought Sid might not come.

"*Police?*" Reshmi squeaked, tension draining out of her

body, leaving her limp with relief. She wiped her perspiring forehead and gave Sid an apologetic smile. "Why didn't you say so? You're going to lock up Pop?" Her lips widened at the thought until her dimples showed.

"Err... not right away." Sid bit his lip, trying not to chuckle when she looked disappointed. He added, "Soon, if I can find evidence."

Mira ran towards Sid with a whoop of excitement and grabbed his legs. "Bad Appa... bad Appa." Now that her sister was smiling, Sid was probably from the good side. Poor kids!

"Is your appa around?"

Reshmi shook her head, her arm curving protectively around her sister's shoulders. "No! I hope he never comes back."

And that told Sid everything he needed to know. He was going to enjoy thrashing that man. He looked at the duo and smiled reassuringly. "If you guys want to get something to eat, go ahead. I'll have a word with your mom."

CHAPTER TWO

"Mrs Chari?"

Jasmine trembled and crawled behind the lustrous marble Jacuzzi, her damp clothing hindering her progress. She cowered against the wall as the tall shadow advanced into the washroom. All she could see were sturdy booted feet and strong denim-clad legs of a physically fit male, and her heart pounded in her chest, knowing she would bleed to death this time.

"Mrs Chari, I'm Sid Chevalier. You called me."

The rescue officer? Peering cautiously through the strands of her wet hair, her body quaked as he dropped to his haunches. His hands were gentle for such a big man, and he towed her from behind the marble tub, his shadowed gaze roaming her bruised face and body. He drew a towel from the handrail, placed it around her slender shoulders, and held the ends together.

"Can you move?"

Her face ached as her torn lips parted in a shaky smile, unaware of how that effort on her battered face affected the officer. His dark eyes burned into hers as if he were promising her he would take care of the man who had messed with her.

Jasmine's head throbbed with pain, sending sharp pins and needles coursing through her battered body as she tried to raise herself to a half-sitting position. Seeing her struggle, Sid instinctively leaned forward, his strong arms enveloping her quivering form as he lifted her gently from the damp floor. As he headed to the master bedroom, she gave a sound of protest, memories of her violation making her shiver in his grip. His soft, soothing voice told her he was there to help her and nothing else.

He flipped the grey duvet hanging on the edge of the bed onto the mattress, concealing the blood-stained white sheet underneath, and then placed her on the bed. Picking a pillow strewn on the floor, he tucked it beneath her head. Drawing a vanity stool near the bed, he settled himself, facing Jasmine.

"Do you have a first-aid kit?"

"Reshmi has already attended to my wounds. Thank you."

"Would you like to tell me what happened?"

Jasmine's hands shook as she reached for a tissue, wiping away the tears streaming down her cheeks. His chocolate brown eyes followed her action, noting her scratched and clawed arms. She avoided his probing gaze, knowing he was waiting for an answer.

What could she say? That her husband raped her night after night? That he often brutalised her? And how would Sunil react when he learnt that his wife had called for help?

From a distance, she could hear her daughters' bubbly chatter. At least they seemed fine. Calling the officer was a positive move; she had set her children's minds at rest if nothing else.

"It doesn't get so rough normally," she said and averted her gaze as his brows started to knit.

The hum of the air conditioner was the only sound in the room, reminding her that Sunil had always provided for them. He wasn't a complete villain, was he? He paid the bills, gave them a luxurious life, and ran the Chari enterprise. Her father always spoke highly of his son-in-law, never once guessing what a pervert he was. But then, her father wasn't any better. She had watched her mother silently suffer his violent temper and infidelities. Her mother never once complained about her husband or let him down to anyone. In public, they were a loving couple.

Could that be the reason Jasmine accepted Sunil's aggression? Following in her mother's footsteps?

So, yes, Sunil had a sinister side, her mother once told Jasmine when she came on a sudden visit from France to attend to an ailing relative in Pondicherry. Her parents had settled in France after having given their daughter in marriage to Sunil Chari along with their company. While in transit, her mother touched base with Jasmine, and noticing the bruises on her daughter, told her in a matter-of-fact voice that no marriage was perfect.

"How often does he beat you, Mrs Chari?"

Tears spilt over Jasmine's nose and cheeks and formed a moist patch on the pillowcase as she stared at the Armani night lamp on the side table. How she wished she could have one peaceful night of sleep. The dark rings under her eyes were evidence of sleepless, restless, fearful nights as she waited for her husband. Would he beat her up while he pounced or leave teeth marks all over her tender skin?

"No marriage is perfect, Officer."

She was doing the same thing that his mother did, Sid thought, as he watched Mrs Chari wiping her eyes. She was protecting her abusive husband and finding excuses for his violence. Didn't they know that these men never changed? That waiting and hoping they would... it was foolish. He wanted to shake some sense into Mrs Chari and urge her to think of her daughters, who would carry the scars of their parents' marriage all through their lives.

"So why did you call me in that case?"

"I was afraid."

"Why were you afraid?"

Jasmine shifted uncomfortably under his hooded gaze, her hands tightening on the towel, holding it protectively against her chest. He leaned down and picked a discarded red *chunni* from the floor and gave it to her so she could cover her torn bodice.

"Reshmi and Mira are all I have. I wanted them out of here."

"And you?"

She shook her head. "I-I n-normally give in to Sunil's d-demands. Last night, he was r-r-rougher than usual. I was sore, h-he wanted me again this morning, I-I couldn't."

"Why do you stay with him, Mrs Chari?"

"I can't leave."

She was just like his mother—a martyr. How many times had he cried in his mother's arms, "*Appā vēṇṭām* (Don't want Daddy)." But she would never hear of it. She preferred to give up her precious son...

No, his mother loved him... loved him enough to help him escape. The Chevaliers took care of Sid and assisted him through his traumatised childhood. He had nothing to reproach his mother for. He should find her and tell her he was grateful she had given him a new start. But *nothing* could replace the love he felt in his mother's arms.

"He'll take away my children."

What was she saying? Did she not know her rights? She looked educated, unlike his mother, who hadn't a clue about women's rights.

"He can't do that, Mrs Chari. The law will not permit it."

"*The law?*" she shrilled and then started to laugh, an empty, lonely expulsion of air that reverberated with sadness. "No law can save me from him, Officer."

"I've helped many women in similar situations."

"Not with a husband like Sunil. He'll not hesitate to take you and your agency apart. You don't know what you're getting into, Officer."

"Mrs Chari—Jasmine... may I call you Jasmine?" He tasted her name on his lips. It felt right.

The damp head gave a slow nod, reluctant hope in her eyes as she listened.

"Single mothers are bringing up their children successfully. There's no reason why it should be different for you. My agency will help you get back on your feet. We'll find a home for you."

"For how long, Officer? I have two minor girls. I've never held a job in my life. Sunil handles all the finances."

"We'll find a way." Sid would have to make some quick arrangements to get them out safely. But first, he needed to clear his head. He stood up. He must talk to Roy and Becka and ask them to arrange a place immediately for Jasmine and her kids.

She grasped his hand as he was about to leave, her cheeks colouring as he looked at her, puzzled.

"Don't leave us, please."

He sank back on the stool and allowed her to keep his hand. Fear was plastered on her face, and he understood her anxiety.

"I was going to get you something to drink, some warm milk, perhaps?"

She released her grip. "I don't want anything, Officer. My children must be hungry." She hauled her tired body and tried to sit. The chunni fell away, and through the torn cotton kameez, he saw the bruises tracing the top of her breasts. Her husband was a beast.

"I'll check on your children." He stood up and hurried out of the room, feeling as if demons were pursuing him.

Sid's mother, too, had lain battered and defenceless while her husband took his pleasure night after night. Then he would go for a drink with his friends. Sid would wait for him to leave and crawl towards his mother. He would sponge her beaten body, and while he did, she would explain that his father wasn't an evil man; he just didn't know what he was doing.

Sid would cry along with her, and as tiny as he was, would tell her they must go to Father Pius. She would cradle his malnourished body against her bosom and reassure him she would find a way. Then that man would stagger into their small hut drunk and accusing, tear Sid away from his mother, and shove him out of the hut. Sometimes, he was allowed to sleep on the porch, but when he was kicked out, Sid would go to the little church run by the missionaries, and Father Pius would shelter him.

Was that why his mother had given him away? Had she feared that her husband would one day kill Sid in a jealous rage?

Sid's smile remained fixed as Mira tugged at his hand, leading him towards the dining hall. The atmosphere was paradoxical—a perfectly set table for four, a display of sophistication and elegance. Forks and knives gleamed, carefully positioned, ready for a meal yet to be shared. But the façade of opulence couldn't overshadow the underlying truth of the situation.

She pushed the thick connecting door between the dining hall and the kitchen and pointed to Reshmi behind the granite countertop of the American-styled kitchen with its state-of-the-art cupboards and plush amenities. As Sid took in the lavish surroundings, his heart couldn't help but ache for these children. The veneer of luxury and material possessions couldn't mask the absence of what they truly desired—peace and happiness. Behind their innocent eyes lay a longing for a sense of normalcy, a childhood free from the shadows that cast a pall over their lives.

At that moment, the aroma of freshly toasted bread wafted through the kitchen. Reshmi asked hesitantly, "Did you speak to Mom?" Her slender shoulders were tense, and her hand had slowed as she spread marmalade on toast.

Sid's heart went out to her. Instead of the happy childhood she should have had, this poor girl was loaded with adult problems.

"I thought I was Superman?" he drawled as he arched a brow. She dumped the toast on the plate, hurried to his side, and threw her arms around his waist with a heartfelt sigh. "You must lock up Pop," she insisted.

Nothing would give Sid greater pleasure than thrashing that tyrant, but whether Jasmine would provide evidence against her husband was doubtful. Sid's mother hadn't, and he was afraid Jasmine wouldn't either.

CHAPTER THREE

Jasmine came to an abrupt halt at the entrance of the dining hall, her eyes settling on her youngest daughter, who was held securely in the officer's arms. His face was tender as he fed Mira toast, and crumbs fell over his T-shirt; however, he did not seem to mind. Reshmi demanded that he feed her, too, and the officer stuffed a large portion of the toast in her mouth, and she crushed it with an exaggerated sound, making them laugh.

Poor Reshmi! She had never enjoyed the love of her father. Sunil had hated her right from birth and would sometimes accuse Jasmine of infidelity. No child of his would go after his throat as Reshmi had on many occasions. The foolish man didn't realise that he had terrified them. It annoyed him, particularly as he adored Mira.

Jasmine watched spellbound as the officer and her children shared bread and laughter. Mira was a friendly child, but not Reshmi; she was suspicious of strangers and didn't allow Jasmine and Mira to mingle with them. But now, Reshmi was talking without reserve to the officer.

Something yanked inside Jasmine. She didn't have this togetherness with Sunil. They lived in an atmosphere of stress, not knowing how the day would end. She couldn't allow her children another minute in this household. She had packed a few clothes for her children and would convince the officer to take them with him.

Reshmi spotted Jasmine leaning against the door and came rushing towards her, eager to include her in the circle of security. Sometimes, Jasmine wondered who the parent was.

Reshmi took the burden in a stride, never complaining that she was denied her childhood. She insisted that she wasn't doing anything out of the ordinary as she loved being with her mother and sister, and it was her duty to protect them.

"We must leave before he comes back, Mom," Reshmi said, looking at the clock on the wall, tension gripping her young frame.

Jasmine's heart pounded in her chest, reminding her of the imminent danger lurking within their home's confines. The sight of the pigeons outside, unaware of the turmoil inside, added a bitter irony to the situation. They had once found solace in caring for those innocent creatures, but today, their safety took precedence.

"Does he come home for lunch?" Sid asked, impatient with himself for having delayed their exit. The thought of Sunil returning during their escape sent a surge of urgency through him. What was the matter with him today? Shouldn't that have been his priority?

"When he beats Mom, he checks on us," Reshmi said.

Sid placed Mira on her feet, and she darted towards Jasmine, wrapped her chubby arms around her, and said, "Mira loves Amma."

Sid felt a sense of tenderness watching mother and daughter. He helped Jasmine to a chair before she slanted to the floor, her weariness evident. He asked Reshmi to fetch a glass of milk for her. He took the glass from Reshmi and held it in front of Jasmine, pressing it to her lips.

"Drink, Jasmine. Do the neighbours know what is happening here?" He turned to Reshmi, knowing he could trust her to give straight answers.

Jasmine leaned back on the chair, her head moving restlessly on the backrest. Talking about Sunil had a way of sapping her energy. She didn't doubt that the officer would help them as Mrs Arora, the neighbour, had vouched for it. But how long could he provide for them? Jasmine would have to take the reins of life and run it at some point. Was she capable of doing that?

And why was she even thinking of it? She knew the odds against such a move.

"Mrs Arora comes by when Pop is not around," Reshmi said. "Only she is allowed."

Jasmine looked at Sid, her anguished eyes pleading with him. "You must not delay, Officer. Take the children and leave before he returns."

Reshmi looked at her mother, startled. Confusion and concern were written on her face, her innocent eyes searching for answers. Was her mother about to send them away? Even Mira seemed to understand something was wrong when she saw tears roll down her *akka's* cheeks. She left her mother's side and hurried to her sister. In her simple way, she said, "Mira loves akka."

Sid's gaze shifted between Jasmine and her children, understanding the gravity of the situation. He knew that the immediate safety of the children was paramount.

"What do you mean, Mom? Reshmi asked in a choked voice, gripping Mira's hand in hers. "We are not going anywhere without you." Her thin body was trembling at the thought of leaving her mother there, alone.

"You know what will happen if all of us leave? Your father will chase after us. At least this way, you will be safe."

Reshmi shook her head, wiping her cheeks with the back of her hand. "How could you want to stay with that monster, Mom? Are you waiting for him to kill you?"

Reshmi's words pierced through the room, carrying a mixture of anger and frustration. Sensing the tension, Mira joined in with tearful cries, her innocent heart unable to comprehend the depths of her father's cruelty.

"He's your father. We're tied for life." Tears streamed down

Jasmine's face as she pulled her daughters closer, seeking solace in their embrace.

Sid felt helpless as he watched the emotional exchange between Jasmine and her daughters. He understood the weight of Jasmine's fears and the complex web that trapped her in an abusive marriage. Yet, Reshmi's plea for her mother's safety resonated strongly. Sunil would get violent when he found out his children had been rescued. He might even harm Jasmine.

The woman was crazy to want to make things work with that brute. He needed, however, to talk to Jasmine and find out why she felt there was no way out. He sent Reshmi and Mira back to the kitchen, asked them to finish their breakfast, and then turned his gaze on Jasmine. Once again, he pressed the glass of milk to her lips.

"Drink, Jasmine."

Reluctantly, Jasmine took small sips, her body responding to the firm pressure of Sid's hand guiding her through each swallow. Sid made sure she drank the last drop. Then he gave her the tissue Reshmi had thoughtfully provided, and she wiped her mouth.

"Now, are you ready to talk?"

A long sigh hissed through her lips as Jasmine met his gaze. "He has our passports with him. We can't go anywhere without his cooperation." Her voice barely carried, weighed down by the gravity of her words.

Sid leaned forward, catching the latter part of her sentence. His mind raced as he processed the information. It was a deliberate tactic by her husband to exert control and ensure his family remained trapped.

"I see. And that is the only reason you can't leave him?" His voice was steady despite the storm of emotions raging within him.

She sat hunched on the chair. She shook her head, causing damp tendrils of hair to cling to the sides of her face, and his heart tightened at the forlorn picture she made.

"What is it that is holding you to him?"

"My children."

"If that is all, Jasmine, we'll help you gain custody. I promise."

"You can't. No one could. I cannot EVER leave him," Jasmine said, her voice laden with despair.

Sid's brows furrowed as he tried to comprehend the depths of her words, sensing there was more beneath the surface.

"Why? Why do you say that? Is there something you are not disclosing?" Sid pressed gently.

She covered her face with unsteady hands, and tears seeped through the gaps of her fingers. "I thought he'd change in time." Her voice came from afar, anguished. She slowly lowered her hands from her tear-streaked face, her gaze meeting his. He could smell roses and fresh soap as she bowed her head. "Mom said he would. Couples had their issues. I must look into my behaviour before pointing fingers at him. My place was with my husband—"

"Provided he treated you well. He didn't," Sid interrupted in a calm and deadly voice, feeling like murdering her mother. "You have every right to walk out of this abusive relationship."

But there's no question of walking out! Jasmine wanted to scream. Sunil had cornered her from all sides. Wasn't that why he was exploiting the situation? He knew that she was stuck with him.

Sid sensed her turmoil and covered her hands with his. "I'm going to get you our best attorneys—"

"It won't work, Officer."

Sid's gaze turned alert as her shoulders started to tremble.

"I signed away my rights."

"What?" he asked with disbelief, leaning closer, his eyes

searching her face.

Jasmine's gaze dropped, her hands trembling with regret.

"The day of our nuptials, Sunil had brought some documents for me to sign. His lawyer was with him. They said that it was a formality—something to do with share transfers and investments. Since Pop made Sunil the CMD of Chari Investments, I believed them."

Sid closed his eyes, beginning to understand where her hopelessness originated. This was even worse than he had imagined.

"A few years into our marriage, I couldn't take the abuse, so I filed for a divorce. It was then I came to know the extent of my stupidity. I'd signed off my rights to everything—property, investments, alimony, and the company. But what makes it even worse is I also lose custody of my children."

Sid gave a low groan. How could she—an educated woman—sign documents without reading them through? He bit on his tongue as he grappled with the reality of the situation. She didn't need his condemnation; she needed his help, and the worst part was that Sid doubted he would be able to do much. Her husband was a powerful man, and now, with that additional document, he would make mincemeat out of Jasmine. Sid could pull strings, undoubtedly, but to nullify a notary stamp paper was practically impossible.

She was looking at Sid now, waiting for his verdict. He gave a grim smile. It was easy to judge people, but given the situation, how could she have suspected that her groom would play dirty, and that, too, on the day of their nuptials? She must have been in the throes of romance. Poor woman!

"We'll work something out. Go and get your things." Sid's mind raced, thinking of any legal avenues they could explore. He had seen enough injustice in his line of work to not let another victim slip through the cracks.

Jasmine nodded, finding comfort in the officer's

unwavering determination. She wiped her tears, a glimmer of hope returning to her eyes.

"You won't send us to a shelter home, will you?"

Sid's gaze softened as he met Jasmine's worried eyes. "I won't send you or your daughters to just any shelter home," he said sincerely. "I will ensure that you are in a safe and secure environment. There are shelter homes specifically designed to cater to the needs of women and children in situations like yours." He thought of the apartment hotel where he had housed Regina and her sons. But that case was different. Regina was a working mother, and her sons were over eighteen.

"Will we be safe there? My daughters are minors. If anything happens to them, I'll never forgive myself."

"It's too short notice to find alternative accommodation, Jasmine, but I'll try. Unfortunately, I live in a bachelor's pad, or I would have accommodated you," he said in clipped tones.

But he could do with their company, a little voice insisted. It was a while since he'd felt so alive. Maybe he could ask Roy or Becka to put them up until...

Until what?

For heaven's sake, Sid! You are the chief operations officer. Your bureau has survived because of sheer persistence, perseverance, and hard work. How could you place yourself at the mercy of your emotions?

Easily! Imagine waking up to a full house, kids running around the place, beautiful Jasmine safe and protected under his roof. It would take his mind off the guilt he felt each time he thought of his mother and his inability to help her.

Suddenly, they heard a loud crash sound as the front door was kicked open and heavy footsteps stomped the corridor. Jasmine froze. Sid urged the panicked woman towards the kitchen, where her children were talking in whispers. Seeing their mother enter so suddenly, Reshmi grabbed Mira and rushed to the corner of the kitchen, her reflexes swift as she and

Mira huddled with their mother between the wall and the huge refrigerator.

"Stay there until I call for you, okay?" he whispered.

Mira began to cry as she saw Sid leave, and he hesitated, wondering if he should stay and console her. But Reshmi placed a hand over her sister's mouth and hissed something in her ear that made her shut up in an instant. Sid straightened, exited the kitchen, and took his position in the dining room behind a pillar partitioning the storeroom from the dining hall. On his right was a tall cream and black unlit Armani lamp.

Sunil Chari stormed into the dining hall, his presence exuding an air of aggression. An aroma of expensive cigars and liquor permeated the atmosphere along with his musky scent as his eyes darted around the room, filled with rage. He was shorter than Sid and slightly on the bulky side. Dressed in formals, he looked every inch the successful businessman. Definitely not a fighter. Or perhaps, he became one only when he dealt with his wife and kids.

"*Jessy!*" Sunil roared. The basilisk's eyes started to search for his victim as if she had displeased him yet again.

Sid watched in horror as Jasmine came stumbling to the hall, closely followed by Mira and Reshmi. He closed his eyes and released his breath. Reshmi placed herself before her mother, poised to leap in case of attack. To Sid, she looked like a young Rajput warrior as she locked eyes with her father. The room seemed to freeze as father and daughter faced each other, a battle of wills between the oppressor and the protector.

A heavy sigh escaped Sid's lips. Why did the Chari family disregard his instructions? Hadn't he been clear enough about ensuring their safety? They seemed to have forgotten he was there, ready to take Sunil apart and crush him to the floor, or better still, shoot him dead. It would solve all Jasmine's problems, although not Sid's.

Sid reached into his pocket, grasping his mobile and

activating the recording device after ensuring the volume was muted. He hung it on the printed lampshade so that he could capture every word and action about to unfold. Keeping to the shadows of the dining hall behind the broad decorative pillar, he crouched, ready to spring at the opportune time.

"Why were you in the kitchen? Preparing something for your dear husband?" Sunil taunted.

His face was flushed, as if he had indulged in a few aperitifs before returning home to check on them.

Seeing her mother quake in fear, Reshmi stepped forward, her voice tinged with defiance. "Hirana has not come today. We were making breakfast."

"Shut up. No one asked you," Sunil pushed Reshmi aside and smiled menacingly at Jasmine. "Going somewhere?" He fingered the loop of the cloth bag hanging on her shoulders, and it slid to the floor soundlessly. "Were you about to leave me, Jessy?" he asked in a soft, dangerous undertone that sent an unsettling shiver down Jasmine's spine. She began to tremble.

"You raise your hand on Mom, I swear I'll kill you," Reshmi said.

Sid's muscles tensed as Sunil threw his head back and laughed. "Get out of the way."

He gave Reshmi a hard shove, sending Reshmi stumbling backwards, his deadly gaze fastening on Jasmine. "A man came here, I was told, a very attractive one. Who is he, Jessy?"

Sid pulled his right arm horizontally across his chest as far as he could, applied pressure with the other arm, and released. He did the same with the other arm. His eyes hadn't left Jasmine, and he swallowed a frustrated growl as she continued to block his access, endangering herself and her children.

If only Jasmine had listened and stayed out of sight, Sid thought in frustration, he would have flattened this character and got them out of there.

Sid stepped out of the shadows, his tall, athletic frame

drawing a startled gasp from Sunil. Dark, sadistic eyes examined Sid, registering his well-toned body, taut face, and steady stride.

"Ah! The man himself!" he spluttered, the angry flush deepening until his face had turned tomato red. "How dare you come to my house when I'm not around?"

Jasmine's terrified gaze darted from Sid to Sunil, her breath coming in short gasps. "He's just moved into the block and came to say hello."

Sid uttered an expletive. What was she doing? She should move out of the way with her children and allow Sid to handle her husband instead of justifying his presence. So engrossed was he in his thoughts that he didn't see the arm that shot out until he saw Jasmine hurtling backwards, colliding with the wall before she crumpled to the floor limply.

Her screams of pain took Sid back in time to his abusive father, and his eyes burned with fury as he grabbed Sunil forcibly, held him in the air for a moment, and flung him against the door connecting the study to the dining hall with all his might. The plump body crashed through and became a part of the debris. On the floor, Sunil lay in a heap, cowering at his feet, his arms rising to cover his face.

Reshmi had left her mother's side and come to Sid's, as if she wanted to see this fight, which was long overdue.

Sid picked Sunil up easily and thrust his face close to his. "The next time you raise your hand on your wife or children, I'll break it. Do you understand?"

Sid wrapped his fist and drew his arm back in one of those boxers' specials when he felt a vice-like grip on his ankle. He looked down, bewildered to see a bleeding Jasmine holding onto his leg and pleading with him to let Sunil go. He tried to free his leg, but her grip tightened.

Did she love this man despite the way he bruised her? He couldn't understand Jasmine, nor could he understand his mother. How could they find compassion for their abusers?

He released Sunil abruptly, and the massive body crashed to the floor.

Reshmi's anger and frustration reached a boiling point when her mother saved her brutal husband from a well-deserved punch. Without hesitation, she approached Sunil's sprawled form with vengeance in her eyes.

"You shouldn't be alive!" she said, her fury intensifying as she kicked him in the groin, unleashing her pent-up anger and seeking a small semblance of justice for her mother. "Men like you should rot in hell."

Sunil's agonised scream filled the air as he writhed in pain.

"That's for all the times you assaulted Mom, you pervert." Reshmi watched him without remorse, her deep-rooted resentment for the years he tortured her mother etched on her face.

"Reshmi!" Jasmine called weakly. Meanwhile, Mira rushed to her mother's side and cradled her head on her lap. She found a box of tissues and began wiping her mother's brow.

Sid didn't say much, still in shock at what nearly happened. Had Jasmine not held him back, he might have killed her husband. He should have more control than that, he thought, as he lifted Jasmine from the floor and held her bruised body, nestling it to his chest. Her bleeding head soaked his shirt, and her tears mingled with blood. He crossed over Sunil, who lay motionless on the floor. Reshmi collected the bag, took her sister's hand, and walked on her father's body, followed by Mira. Sunil gave another howl.

"You'll regret this, bitch." He summoned the strength to carry his voice through. Enough to make Jasmine tremble in Sid's arms. "You'll never get custody of Mira."

Mira paused and looked over her shoulder. Sunil was calling out to her, but Reshmi dragged Mira along with them, and the little girl broke down in loud wails. Sid waited for Mira to reach him, swept the little toddler off the floor effortlessly, and held mother and daughter in his arms. Reshmi walked beside him like she was his guardian and had pledged her life to him.

Sid's heart constricted as the four of them entered the elevator. With each passing floor, they moved closer to a new chapter, one where they would seek justice, healing, and a life free from the shadows of abuse.

CHAPTER FOUR

Jasmine's hair ripped out of the loose knot and slapped against her face as the silver convertible clipped on NH4. Tall glass structures and malls swept past them as regular morning traffic competed for space. Horns blared as pedestrians tried to traverse the broad roads, some running past as the ongoing vehicles refused to slow down.

Reshmi and Mira were safely buckled behind and were squealing with excitement. Anyone would think they were off on a joy ride and not escaping from a dire situation. Sunil had telephoned security personnel at the gates, but fortunately, they had zoomed out of the parking lot of Residency Towers seconds before the automated barricades shut.

What a close call that was!

How enraged Sunil must be. Jasmine had never defied him and had always been the obedient wife. He was probably placing the blame on Reshmi and the officer. Her head ached with all the bashing she'd been receiving; however, she didn't allow Sid to stop at the hospital. There was no time for that. Sunil must have sent his personnel after them. And anyway, Jasmine's body had become immune to beatings. For the last decade, she'd been assaulted practically every day, so one more to the list wasn't going to make a difference.

"Do you want the roof back on?" Sid turned to look at her as she tucked her hair beneath the collar of her tunic, preventing it from flying around her. But a few strands came loose and plastered themselves to his face.

Gesturing towards the back seat where Reshmi and Mira were gleefully squealing, Jasmine couldn't help but smile. It had been far too long since she had seen her children so excited and carefree.

"Don't want to spoil their fun."

Sid shot a glance at the duo, and he had to agree they were indeed enjoying themselves. "Didn't Sunil take you out?"

Jasmine sighed, her gaze fixed on the road ahead. "He provided us a chauffeur. In all honesty, we preferred to be alone. It was less tense that way. Sunil would always pick on Reshmi, even when she did nothing to provoke him. I would be torn between my daughter and my husband—not that Reshmi expected my support. She advised me to take his side so he wouldn't hurt me. It's heartbreaking how well our children knew their father."

His eyes didn't leave the road as he placed his hand on hers and gave it a comforting squeeze. Between the lines, he read something there; he could be wrong, but it felt like she preferred that he left them on their own.

Unaware of how attractive he looked to the woman who had never tasted gentleness, Sid turned and smiled at her, loosening his grip on her hand and bringing it back on the wheel. She made a sound of protest, and he smiled again and brought it back on hers. Then he brought her hand to the wheel and imprisoned it under his warm palm.

Jasmine's gaze shied away from the officer as her cheeks started to heat. It was a long time since she had received any attention from a man, let alone one as handsome as this officer. She hoped she was not developing romantic feelings for him as that would complicate their already complicated situation. She couldn't afford to let her guard down and risk getting hurt again. Her focus had to be on protecting herself and her children.

Reshmi was watching her. Jasmine felt her warm breath on the back of her neck. She knew her daughter was curious.

All she had seen was screaming, shouting, and beating—no tenderness. Seeing her mother finding solace in the officer's presence ignited hope in her heart. Jasmine drew her hand away, and Sid arched a brow, glancing at her flushed face. She fidgeted with the hem of her kameez, her fingers nervously tracing the fabric as she attempted to distract herself from the awkwardness of the moment.

The vehicle nosed through the traffic-ridden four-way road, overtaking two BMWs and a Mercedes. Reshmi and Mira cheered as if Sid was competing in a thrilling race. Sid grinned over his shoulders at the enthusiastic girls, the tension that had enveloped the car seeming to dissipate at that moment, replaced by a sense of exhilaration.

"Do you guys want to eat something?" he asked, raising his voice to be heard against the loud klaxons and traffic noise.

"Can I have a Big Mac?" Reshmi asked with a cheeky grin. Jasmine shot Reshmi an irritated glance. She pretended not to notice and turned towards her sister. "What does Mira want?"

Whether it was Reshmi's gentle tone or sudden melancholy, Mira's lips curled outwards.

"Mira wants Appa," she said with a loud wail as tears seeped through the tightly shut lids.

Reshmi exchanged a startled glance with her mother as Mira continued to bawl, rubbing her eyes with her closed fists. "Appaaaaaaaa... Mira wants Appa."

Sid looked worriedly at Jasmine and saw panic on her face. Her hands fluttered to her throat somewhat indecisively. What were they going to do if Mira didn't stop fretting? Would she have to go back to that madman?

"Jasmine," Sid called softly, and she turned her troubled gaze to his. "Are you having second thoughts?" Hell! What was he supposed to do now? Drive the family back to their residence and ask Sunil to forgive them?

She bent her head, not knowing how to answer. The

thought of returning to Sunil was terrifying. She turned and looked at Reshmi, who was consoling Mira, an arm around her shaking shoulders.

"If we go back, Appa will beat Amma again. Do you want that?" Reshmi asked Mira.

Sid held his breath, waiting for the verdict. He knew without a doubt that if the child insisted, Jasmine would return to that maniac. She turned her head to gauge the situation, and Sid hoped Reshmi would solve it.

"He will beat Reshmi, too, and the police will take Uncle Sid away."

Mira's sobs became less intense, and the tremors gradually ceased. She lay her head on Reshmi's shoulders and said with childish insistence, "Bad Appa... bad Appa."

Reshmi caught Sid's eye in the rear-view mirror. *You can count on me,* she seemed to say.

They stopped at McDonald's, picked up their order, and continued to their destination. The city gradually gave way to open landscapes, the traffic thinning as they ventured further away from the urban chaos.

Sid's need for privacy made him procure a villa far from the maddening crowd. The moment he had seen the cluster of villas uphill with their private pools and palm trees, he hadn't been able to resist. He had wanted a compact villa where security was tight. He didn't mind the long drive to the office and back. What he wanted was peace.

Reshmi and Mira devoured their burgers while Sid took a bite of his chicken sandwich. Jasmine tucked her sandwich in her bag. Suddenly, she seemed far away in thought and wasn't talking much. Sid veered off the main road, taking a right at a junction. The surroundings grew sparse, with only a few scattered buildings dotting the deserted highway. Jasmine's gaze seemed fixated on a run-down two-level motel they passed, its faded sign swinging gently in the breeze.

"Drop us off at that motel," she said.

Sid slammed on the brakes, bringing the car to a screeching halt. She reached down and retrieved her cloth bag, holding it in her hands tightly, and looked at Reshmi. A tremor ran through Reshmi, her apprehension evident as she shook her head in silent refusal.

Sid's eyes widened in horror as he processed Jasmine's intention. His body tensed, and a shiver ran down his spine at the sight of the trucks parked outside and the rowdy voices that pierced the otherwise silent night.

"Surely, you don't mean that? It's no place for a woman— let alone minor girls. I thought that was why you didn't want to go to a rescue home?"

Jasmine's heart ached with conflicted emotions as she wrestled with the difficult choice. She knew that going with Sid held its own uncertainties, especially considering her children's growing attachment towards him. What if he had a family of his own? What if their connection only complicated matters further?

"It's all I can afford right now, Officer! I don't have much on me."

"Sleazy characters go there, Jasmine."

Her shrill laughter was all he got as an answer, but he understood the message. After undergoing her husband's manhandling, she could take on the seediest of characters.

"I know you mean well, Officer," she said as she held his glance, emotion clouding her tone and making her want to cry. "But you've done your part and rescued us. I need to learn to stand on my feet starting right now."

Sid's jaw tightened, concern flashing in his eyes as Jasmine signalled to Reshmi to gather Mira and leave the car. He felt helpless as he watched them, his hands gripping the steering wheel tightly, his mind filled with worry for their safety.

"We should go with Sid, Mom," Reshmi said, her tone laced with unease as she looked around them. "This place seems unsafe, and that monster will come after us."

Let Jasmine deal with her daughter. Sid was happy Reshmi was seeing the folly in what her mother was suggesting. Mira was trying to follow the conversation and grasped a new word, 'monster', that she repeated to herself, giggling each time she didn't get it right.

Jasmine locked eyes with Reshmi. "We've always managed on our own, remember? You, I, and Mira." She hoped Reshmi would not kick up a fuss. They had already troubled the officer enough, and Sunil would attack his agency if they stayed longer with him. Surely Reshmi should know that?

"Not this time, Mom. We need help. If we're alone, he'll take us back. I don't want to go back, Mom. I'm tired. I can't take it anymore. *I can't.*"

All Sid could think of as he jumped into the back seat was that the strong and courageous Reshmi had broken down. He shot Jasmine a glance that told her what he thought. Her shoulders hunched, and her head dropped forward, making him feel like he was dealing with three children. He placed his strong arms around the girls as he squeezed himself between them.

"I'm not going anywhere without you."

Reshmi raised a tearful gaze to him, and suddenly, Sid was seeing himself as he had been those years ago, crying as he held on to his mother's waist. *Don't let them take me, Amma*, he had wept as the Chevaliers pried his thin arms from around his mother's waist. His mother had stood there like a statue as they took him away, not even turning to watch him go. Sid had often wondered whether it was because she wouldn't have been able to walk away had she turned back and looked at him.

He felt a soft hand touch his face and realised his cheeks were damp.

"Promise?"

Jasmine turned and gave Reshmi a hard stare as Reshmi held her palm out. But her daughter wasn't meeting her glance. Her tear-soaked eyes were on Sid. He placed a hand over hers and drew a cross. "I promise."

"We can stay with you?"

"Until I arrange another accommodation," he inserted hurriedly as he saw opposition rising from Jasmine's stiff posture. It was difficult pleasing mother and daughter.

Reshmi leapt on him with an excited shriek and displaced Mira, who had been curled on his lap. Mira fought her way back, her tiny arms winding around his neck. "Mira loves Uncle Sid."

Jasmine looked out of the window as Sid took the wheel once again. Sid understood her silence. She had been taking care of her daughters all this while and was probably feeling betrayed. But she must know her daughters were afraid and had turned to Sid as he represented security.

Mira pointed in the distance to an unusual sight of traditional nomads with their hundreds of sheep in search of lush green pastures. She sang 'Baa Baa Black Sheep', pointing to the clouds, but instead of saying *black*, she said *white* sheep. Reshmi corrected her, but the little girl explained that these sheep were white.

Sid enjoyed their chit-chat; however, he felt guilty, as if he'd stolen their affection. He had to discuss the matter with Roy and Becka tomorrow; the latter was going to be mad. Becka had hinted several times that she would give anything to move in with Sid.

If only he hadn't given in to Becka's charms that night when she'd come to his place unannounced. He had been vulnerable after having a few drinks and had become emotional while discussing his mother. Becka had been such a great listener, and he had found comfort in her arms.

"Do you know what you're doing?"

Sid was drawn abruptly from his thoughts, and his head

swung sideward to see a pair of accusing eyes glittering with tears.

"We don't need you. We don't need any man."

Sid held back his ready response. He was beginning to feel hounded by this woman's tantrums. He was trying to be fair here, but he couldn't seem to please her in whatever he did. Of course, his job should have ended with the rescue, and it would have, had he not met these adorable kids. They reminded Sid of how helpless he had been those years ago, with nowhere to go and no one to stand by him.

His jaw tautened. "Fine, I got your message loud and clear. Now, get mine. I'm tired. I can't look for a place right now, and you don't want to go to a rescue home. So tonight, you and your children will stay at my place."

He left her to her thoughts, refusing to admit she had upset him. He was going out of his way to keep them safe, risking his reputation and that of the agency to help them, and she didn't seem to appreciate it. Why the heck was he breaking his head over her?

He drove into the five-acre property with its multiple terraces, pools, and private spas. His villa was one of the few with a built-in fireplace, which came in handy during winter. He loved the tiled roof and spacious portico that let him relax in front of the pool in privacy.

He could feel Jasmine's gaze but didn't acknowledge it. There were so many things he had to do, he thought, as he passed through the security gates. Mashraf was on duty. He must leave instructions to watch for suspicious movements around the villa. He had promised the kids he would protect them and Jasmine, too. He had to keep his word.

Jasmine cleared her throat, and he looked at her enquiringly, his brow arched. What was it this time? Did she not like the isolation? Was she going to kick up a fuss?

"I'm sorry," she said so softly that he almost missed it. He shrugged and continued to drive without saying anything. "I've never known gentleness in a man."

He glanced at her earnest face and found his heart stirring once again. Reshmi leaned over the seat and added, "What Mom is trying to say is that her husband never bothered about her. Even when she was sick, he did not take her to the doctor—"

"Reshmi!" Jasmine interrupted, glaring at her. "I'm sure Officer Chevalier has other things on his mind than my marital relationship."

"Bad Appa, bad Appa," Mira chirped.

"Stop it, both of you!" Jasmine shouted.

Sid's lips tilted upwards. "On the contrary, I need all the information I can get to build a strong case, Jasmine. Your husband is going to come after us. And please call me Sid." He met Reshmi's eyes in the rear-view mirror and winked. She winked back.

Jasmine felt an odd sense of security, although she wouldn't admit it. For once, she didn't need to worry that no one cared about them. Officer Sid seemed to care; at least, that was the impression he gave. Mrs Arora had told her about the many women he had rescued, one of them being her niece Rupa. Thanks to him, Rupa had found the courage to stand up to her husband and fight for her rights. She was now in Canada and doing well for herself.

But Rupa didn't have a husband like Sunil, she reminded herself. That was no idle threat Sunil had issued. He would make sure they paid. The officer had no idea of what he had got himself into.

Her eyes secretly studied his attractive profile as he manoeuvred the car through the gates. He suddenly gripped the steering wheel, and her heart leapt to her throat. Had Sunil caught up with them? She peeped through the window.

A very stylish-looking woman in her late twenties was straightening from her leaning position against the wall as the car came to a halt. She wore faded jeans, a tight top, and large-framed sunglasses.

Sid slid out and came around to open the door for Jasmine. He then left her to it as he hurried in the direction of the woman. The lady strode towards the car, tall and gorgeous, pushing the sunglasses over her head, her subtly made-up face and azure eyes turning enquiringly towards Jasmine and her daughters.

CHAPTER FIVE

Jasmine exhaled noisily as Sid called out to them. This was exactly what she had been trying to avoid. Reshmi came to stand beside Jasmine, and her heart went out to Reshmi as she looked doubtful for the first time.

"Who is she?" Reshmi asked in dismay as the woman extended her arms towards Sid.

Jasmine kept a firm hold on Reshmi. Mira's head rested on her shoulder, and her chubby arms were around Jasmine's neck.

The vibrant hues of blooming flowers added bursts of colour to the meticulously maintained garden. Fragrant roses danced in the gentle breeze, their velvety petals inviting admiration. The air was alive with the melodies of chirping birds, their joyful songs creating a serene atmosphere.

She couldn't say how many trees surrounded the officer's villa, but he had made sure there were enough to prevent prying eyes. He was a very wealthy man by the looks of it and valued his privacy. She knew the prices of property as her father was in the real estate business and had often had discussions on the subject with his daughter before he married her off to Sunil. This piece of land would put a hole in even a rich man's pocket.

"Perhaps his wife," she said to Reshmi, thinking it was time to burst her daughter's bubble. But Jasmine's heart took a nosedive at the thought. Sid was a handsome and wealthy man. How could she have imagined he was single?

"He's not married, Mom," Reshmi said with such confidence that it was as if she'd known the officer for ages.

"They don't need to be married these days," Jasmine retorted in dry tones.

"He wouldn't have invited us to stay with him if she was his partner."

Jasmine looked at her daughter, knowing that she'd taken to Sid. She tipped Reshmi's chin upwards and said in soft, stern tones, "Don't build hopes, Reshmi, that he's going to fall for me and we're going to live happily… that only happens in fairy tales."

A stain of red crept into Reshmi's face, and a pair of guilty eyes evaded hers. Jasmine had hit the nail on the head, and it was evident that her daughter was building hopes of having the officer in their lives.

"I'm married to your father, Reshmi. Officer Chevalier is helping us out of a bad situation, not taking us on as his family. Remember that."

Reshmi started to struggle in her hold, and Jasmine let go of her shoulders as she didn't want her to hurt her. But that was a mistake. With one tug, Reshmi wrenched herself away and ran towards Sid and the woman. Jasmine looked on in horror as Reshmi darted to the officer's side and tucked her hand in his as if he belonged to them.

Something snapped inside Jasmine. She couldn't bear to watch her daughter fight for Sid's attention. What must he be thinking of them? And his partner? What must she be making of the situation?

But Sid wasn't ignoring Reshmi; he was introducing her to his lady friend as if it were normal that Reshmi should hold his hand.

What was he doing to them? How had he managed in such a short time to win their hearts?

The woman gave Reshmi a look that should have put her in her place, but Reshmi, being the bold brat she was, out-stared the woman until she looked away.

Jasmine trailed slowly behind them, carrying Mira in her arms. She avoided eye contact with the officer as he seemed to have enough on his plate. Poor man! God knows how he was explaining the situation to his partner.

On seeing Jasmine close behind, he held his arms open for Mira, but Jasmine shook her head, refusing to part with her. One glance at his stunning lady friend, and she knew she'd made the right decision. Rebecca, the woman Sid fondly introduced to Jasmine, seemed to force a smile, but the sparks in her eyes made it clear that she wasn't pleased with their uninvited guests.

Sid swiped his electronic card at the door; it glided open, revealing a spacious, elegant, carpeted hall. The furniture exuded a contemporary, minimalistic style, leaving space for easy movement. As the shutters gracefully ascended, the house was illuminated with a spectacular garden view. Sunlight swept inside as a major part of the villa was fashioned in toughened natural glass.

Reshmi, who was normally a well-behaved child, darted under his arm and charged into the hall with a shriek. Jasmine closed her eyes and sighed. Trust Reshmi to misbehave at such a crucial moment. The woman's face had turned red, and she whispered something to Sid, probably enquiring about the badly brought-up child.

Jasmine decided to stay in the portico with Mira, and later, when she got a chance, she would screw Reshmi's ears. She had a feeling her daughter was doing her worst to disturb Sid's lady friend.

"I hope you know what you're doing, boss," Rebecca hissed beneath her breath.

The trees outside were illuminated artfully from below, giving Sid's garden a charming, almost Christmassy ambience at dusk.

Sid paid no heed to the simmering resentment emanating from Becka. "They need a roof, Becka."

"And you need to have your head examined," she said, her face tightening in annoyance as she saw Reshmi leaping on the black leather canapé as if she were testing the springs.

Sid struggled not to laugh and caught Becka's arm as she took a step towards Reshmi. "Not now, Becka. I'm going for a shower. Make them feel comfortable," he instructed his beautiful and enraged Becka. Sid's eyes searched for Jasmine and found her seated in the basket chair swing on the portico. She was cradling Mira in her arms, gently rocking her to sleep.

Sid's heart ached as he watched the forlorn figure staring sightlessly into the distant horizon. Was she regretting leaving her husband? Had Sid made a mistake with this case? Had he let his emotions overrule his head and rescued a woman who didn't want to be rescued? He could feel the burning intensity of Becka's blue eyes on his back as he strolled to the portico. He touched Jasmine's shoulder, offering her a reassuring smile. He carefully lifted the sleeping child and carried Mira to the guest room.

Becka's mouth had fallen open in astonishment as he exited the room. When he returned, Sid addressed her in dry tones, "Close your mouth, Becka! I just put her to bed so she can sleep without disturbance."

"And *her*?" Becka said, gesturing to Reshmi, who had now climbed on the bar stool and was spinning on its axis with a goofy grin.

The sleek, lacquered black bar with its six bar stools occupied a significant part of Sid's lounge. Behind it stood a transparent glass cabinet with black and gold shelves that illuminated upon opening.

Sid's lips curved in a wistful smile, the sight of Reshmi and the simple pleasure she was deriving making him want to join her. "You leave her alone," he said in a tone timbered with warning.

Rebecca nodded, trying to hide her bitterness. She didn't

like Reshmi and the way she had interrupted a private conversation and claimed Sid. She didn't like how Sid had responded as if Reshmi had a right to feel that way. Nor did she like the woman with the almond-shaped eyes and the lost-girl look who had neatly inserted herself into Sid's life.

She was going to find a way to get the Chari family out of Sid's villa and out of his life. For once, Roy was on her side. When Sid had texted that he was going to shelter the Chari family, Roy had instructed Becka to rush to Sid's place and find out what was happening. Their boss rarely took such risks, and Roy couldn't help but wonder what Sid was even thinking, especially when he knew who he was dealing with.

Rebecca headed to the kitchen, trying not to think of arson as she turned on the electric kettle and set the tray for the guests. Sid had some cheek asking her to attend to them, considering Rebecca had been trying to live with him for ages. Sometimes, she questioned why she continued to chase after a man who had made it clear he didn't want her. But then, she would recall that one night she had seduced him, and a feeling of purity would wash over her. In her mind, that single night with Sid had cleansed her of the stains of her sordid past.

No more was Rebecca tormented by nightmares of her stepdad coming into her room and forcing her to have sex with him. Her mother had never believed her, always thinking she was cooking up stories to break them up. It never crossed her mind that Rebecca was thirteen and her husband was a grown-up middle-aged man lusting after an innocent body. Rebecca had fled home and sought refuge in a convent until she turned eighteen. While there, she studied hard, earned a scholarship, and specialised in criminology. Alongside her major in investigative science, Rebecca undertook rigorous training with some of the best martial arts experts. Her hard work paid off as she completed her studies successfully, and after years of training, discipline, and passing through various levels, she had reached this prestigious milestone: a black belt in martial arts.

No man could touch her now... not unless she allowed him.

She strode out of the kitchen, her silky mane falling gracefully onto her shoulders. Her striking cobalt eyes and sculpted cheekbones added to her undeniable beauty, a fact that hadn't escaped the attention of every man who crossed her path. However, there was one man who seemed immune to her charms: Sid. He seemed to seek Rebecca only when he required her professional services, never acknowledging the magnetic pull she felt towards him. She couldn't help but sigh in exasperation. Sid was her ideal man, the one she had set her heart on since their very first encounter. His slumberous eyes had cast a spell on Rebecca, making her feel special in a way no one else could. Yes, Sid was her kind of man.

Through the corner of her eye, she noticed Reshmi looking at her, still perched on the bar stool. But now the spin had slowed to a halt. She leapt off the stool, hurried towards her mother, and sat beside her. She faced Rebecca with a defiant stare, watching as she laid the table.

If Rebecca wasn't annoyed with their presence, she might have admired the girl's support towards her mother. In these days, when children were not necessarily grateful to their parents, Reshmi gave the impression that she took care of her mother. Even now, her arm was around her mother's hunched shoulders as if she sensed her vulnerability and was reassuring her.

Rebecca focused on the silent woman bent before her, appearing as if the weight of the world rested squarely on her shoulders.

"Do you know your husband has put the police on your trail, Mrs Chari?" Rebecca broke the silence, dropped the information casually, and leaned back in her chair to watch.

The teacup clattered on the saucer, causing the hot liquid to spill over its rim as Mrs Chari placed it on the table. A pang of guilt gripped Rebecca; she hadn't intended to frighten the woman, but Mrs Chari needed to understand the potential dangers they faced by staying under Sid's roof. She looked out of the French window, where noisy squirrels chattered as they scampered up and down the palm tree trunks in search of food, some daringly leaping onto the fronds.

Reshmi gave her mother's stooped shoulders a tight squeeze. "I'm with you," she whispered and turned her dark, intelligent gaze on Rebecca. The intense stare might have rattled someone less experienced than Rebecca, who was used to difficult situations.

"We're used to being chased by the police. They are *his* friends."

Jasmine glanced at Reshmi, willing her not to antagonise Sid's partner. But Reshmi's defiant eyes said: *If you aren't going to fight for Sid, don't stop me. He is ours, given to us by God to make up for the love we've never had.*

"Look, we didn't want to come here," Jasmine began somewhat nervously, "but Sid..." She closed her eyes and groaned. Why did she refer to him as Sid? She had called him 'officer' till now. She was only making the situation worse. For now, the blue stare had turned hard and suspicious. Jasmine cleared her throat and said again, "Officer Chevalier insisted we stay tonight as it was too late for other arrangements."

"I see." Rebecca pursed her lips. It almost seemed like Mrs Chari was silently apologising for her daughter's apparent arrogance. As Rebecca observed Reshmi, she felt a growing sense of unease. The young brat was a quick thinker and couldn't be easily intimidated. The challenge of extricating this family from Sid's life suddenly seemed much more daunting. How in god's name was she going to accomplish this?

"Did Sunil contact your office?" Mrs Chari asked.

Rebecca nodded, her expression serious. "He threatened to bring charges on Sid for assault, kidnap, and many more offences." She lifted the cup and sipped, leaving them to digest the consequences of the threats. "I don't have to tell you what we stand to lose if he does that."

Jasmine felt the prison gates close around her. She knew what Sunil could do and didn't need to be told of his destructive nature. Sid had taken him on and swept Sunil's family out of his reach. That wouldn't sit well on Sunil, who was proud of his authority. She won't let him hurt the officer and the agency. What did she have to lose anyway? She had lived this dreary life for several years. She would go back to him.

Reshmi was observing Jasmine and saw the trapped look on her face. Reshmi hunched her shoulders and looked away in disappointment. Jasmine felt sorry for her. Reshmi would stand to lose the most as Sunil would separate her from them. He had always said he would send Reshmi back to France to stay with her grandparents as she was a bad influence on Jasmine and Mira.

Reshmi shook her head, rose, and strode across to where Rebecca was seated. As she walked, she pulled out her phone from her pocket, scrolled down to whatever she was looking for, and handed the phone to Rebecca. Rebecca raised an eyebrow, her eyes locking with Reshmi's dark gaze. She took the phone and swiped the images one after the other.

How had Reshmi managed to get the woman's attention? Jasmine wondered. But whatever Reshmi was showing Rebecca was turning the lady's beautiful face into a mask of fury.

Could it be something to do with Jasmine? She wouldn't put it past her daughter to have taken pictures of her and Sunil.

Rebecca had turned pale now and was trying to regain her composure. Her eyes found Jasmine and stayed on her. "How did you survive, Mrs Chari?" Her voice sounded strangely concerned. Gone were the cold blue eyes that had been snapping at Jasmine. Now, she seemed somewhat in a trance.

Jasmine looked at her feet, ashamed to admit she had been

afraid. Afraid of what Sunil would do to her and her daughters if they escaped.

"I didn't have a choice."

"He's a madman. He needs to be behind bars."

"He won't get there. He's too powerful."

"Mrs Chari, you don't know Sid. He's never lost a case. He will bring this man to his knees. In the meantime, you have to be strong and resist when he threatens you."

"I stand to lose everything—including the custody of my children if I go against him."

"Was that why you stayed?"

Whatever resentment Rebecca had initially felt was slowly replaced by rage, a violent rage against the male kingdom. Men like Jasmine's husband, Sid's father, and Rebecca's stepfather shouldn't live to torture another woman.

If she thought Reshmi was finished, she was wrong. She showed Rebecca video clips of her father attacking her mother. Rebecca gasped aloud as she saw Sunil grab Jasmine and punch her in the stomach, his nails tearing into her face and neck, teeth clamping on her breasts.

Jasmine suddenly rose and fled to a small corner, where she flopped on the marble floor, hugging her knees to her chest. It was the last attack of Sunil's that was the most painful, even more now, since Reshmi had witnessed it, too. No wonder Reshmi hated Sunil. She had been a secret witness to his atrocities.

CHAPTER SIX

Sid ran out of the shower, hair dripping wet, wearing only a bathrobe as he burst into the lounge on hearing Jasmine's piercing screams. His brows pleated as he saw only Becka and Reshmi. No signs of Jasmine or her brute of a husband.

"What is it?" He lowered his head to see what they were watching, Becka, having reduced the volume. Colour drained from Sid's face as he saw Sunil tearing Jasmine's nightwear, his nails leaving scars on her fair body. Her screams for mercy were too much for Sid, and he moved away and steadied his breathing. Then suddenly, his eyes bounced to the lone figure huddled in the corner, and he rushed towards Jasmine.

"Jasmine?" Sid's voice was gentle, his gaze fixed on her, trying to dispel the lingering shadows of her nightmare. She looked at Sid with blank eyes. "Jasmine, you're with us now." He knelt and held her shoulders gently. "He can't hurt you anymore. I won't let him." His arm encircled her back while the other slid under her knees as he lifted her from the floor. He carried her to the canapé, where he placed her on the comfortable leather couch and sat beside her. "I promise."

Jasmine's sobs were as frightened as those of her daughters earlier in the car when Sid had comforted them. She burrowed in Sid's protective embrace for the first time, seeking refuge, and his arms clamped around her. She wet his bare chest with her warm tears and wiped her damp cheeks against the soft texture of his bathrobe.

When Sid lifted his head, he saw Becka hastily avert her gaze but not quickly enough to conceal her emotions. Her eyes swam with betrayal. He could convince himself all he wanted that he had not led Becka on, but she had taken that one night very seriously. He realised that now.

Becka tucked Reshmi's mobile in her pocket, probably reversing her opinion of Reshmi, but then, Sid had sized up Reshmi from the moment she had come at him with a golf club in her hand, ready to knock him down. His heart had shifted when Reshmi's fearless black eyes had met his. Behind that show of courage, there had been a little girl fighting to save her mother and sister. It was at that instant Sid knew he wanted to be their hero.

Thinking of that rescue now, a troubling thought flashed across Sid's mind, and he slapped his forehead, a groan of frustration emitting deep inside him. He had wanted a video of Sunil attacking Jasmine, not knowing that Reshmi had enough evidence against her father. However, he had forgotten to retrieve it. Sid's mobile phone was still hooked to the lampstand at Jasmine's residence. Damn! How could he have been so careless? Even though he had silenced the volume, if Sunil discovered it, there was no telling what harm he could inflict with access to Sid's private files.

Reshmi came towards Sid now and halted in front of them. Jasmine moved out of his arms as she, too, felt his tension.

Jasmine was somewhat uncomfortable that she had practically thrown herself on Sid and cried like a baby. She must remember she was a grown woman with kids and had to take care of them. There was no time for such luxuries as tears.

Sid let his head drop back on the couch, releasing a long-suppressed breath. "I've left my mobile behind," he admitted regretfully. "I needed to capture a video, not realising that Reshmi had gathered enough evidence. I hooked my phone to the lampstand in your dining hall. In that confusion, I completely forgot about it. Sunil will have access to my private files."

Jasmine's face turned sickly grey as she staggered to her feet, her body weighed down by the news. What could be worse than this? Sunil would make a meal out of that information. He would ruin Sid. She must leave. Sid did not deserve Sunil's wrath. How she wished she'd never picked up that phone and got this poor officer involved.

With her mind set, Jasmine made her way slowly towards the guest room. The thought of leaving the security of that place was terrifying, but she had to do it. She shouldn't burden this officer and his partner and jeopardise rescue operations. She picked the sleeping Mira from the bed and hugged her to her chest. In the hall, Reshmi was waiting for her, and this time, without argument.

"Where do you think you're going?" Sid asked, bewildered, watching Jasmine with Mira in her arms and Reshmi beside her, heading towards the exit. "Jasmine, *arrête!*"

Rebecca looked anxiously from the Chari family to her boss. She hadn't been working for Sid all these years without learning about his moods. He needed to be reassured, and she wished she could do it, but there was too much on the plate already, and this additional piece of news was the icing on the cake. Rebecca did not have to ask Sid how he managed to leave his mobile behind because, after seeing those videos, even Rebecca might have erred. Mrs Chari was one strong woman to have survived that brutal husband of hers for so many years.

Rebecca's heart yearned for Sid to show her a fraction of the attention he was showing Mrs Chari, but apart from that night when they'd made love, her boss had never looked at her in that way.

Rebecca pushed the thought to the back of her mind, her professionalism at the forefront, and said, "I'll go there tomorrow. Draw me the plan of the house and the location of your phone. Hopefully, it hasn't been found yet."

"Don't be silly, Becka. I'll deal with it," Sid said.

Jasmine's eyes glistened with tears. The woman was brave and in love, willing to sacrifice herself for her man. Did Sid return Rebecca's devotion? Jasmine felt like the interloper. Sid and Rebecca were young, uncomplicated, and right for each other. They had hearts of gold, ready to go the extra mile for a stranger. It was time to leave them alone, return to her tainted life, and allow these young lovers their space.

"I'm going back."

Sid jerked as if Jasmine had slapped him. He rose and went towards her, his face like a thundercloud. Reshmi stepped forward, her young body poised to leap, her eyes telling him that she might have pledged loyalty to him but not when it came to her mother.

Sid halted in his tracks, taken aback by Reshmi's ferocious gaze, realising that she had misunderstood his quick strides. "I'm not going to harm your mom. *Merde*! How can you think that? Haven't I proved myself to you?"

"Stay where you are!"

Sid let out a long, tired breath, his gaze falling on the young Rajput warrior, not knowing whether to applaud her or shake her. Even Becka seemed astonished as she came to his side. She made a sound in her throat, and they exchanged glances. She seemed to say: *Never expected that, did you, boss?*

"If you go back to your father, there's no telling how he will react."

"He's not my father!" Reshmi said, glancing upwards, as if waiting for Jasmine's verdict.

Sid felt like he was facing the biggest battle of his life as Jasmine stood there indecisively. Finally, she lifted her troubled gaze to his.

"My husband is a dangerous opponent, Officer. If he finds your phone before we do, you are finished. We'll go back and contact you from there, and as soon as the situation settles, we'll escape."

"You won't be lucky this time," Rebecca interjected grimly.

They looked so beautiful together, Jasmine thought, hardening her resolve to leave. She was touched that the young woman, despite her love for Sid and her possessiveness, was trying to help her.

"You forget your husband has tasted defeat, Mrs Chari. He will tighten security. You won't get another opportunity. It's a miracle you've survived this far."

Jasmine ran a shaking hand against her forehead and looked at Rebecca. "But the phone... how do we get it if I don't go back?"

"I'll go there tomorrow. I've done stuff like this before. We can build a strong case against your husband with all the evidence," Rebecca stated, meeting Sid's gaze. He gave a reluctant nod.

Jasmine looked at them and knew they had come to an agreement, but she still couldn't let Rebecca go there alone. "Let me go with you. I know the location. We'll find it faster."

"I won't hear of it," Sid interrupted with a stern glance at Jasmine. "What about your children? Who'll take care of them if anything happens to you? I'll go with Becka. We've worked together and know how to handle these kinds of stressful situations."

"I think I'll take Reshmi with me," Rebecca said as her thoughtful gaze rested on the intelligent face. She could use that quick, sharp mind of Reshmi's. "That is if it's okay with you, Mrs Chari. Reshmi is agile. We can move fast."

Jasmine started to tremble at the thought of Reshmi walking into Sunil's den. What if he trapped her? What if he locked her up and tortured her? She couldn't do that to Reshmi. She opened her mouth to protest, but Reshmi cut in, her eyes gleaming.

"Will I be in police uniform?"

Sid's lips twitched as he traded glances with Becka. He had still not clarified his exact designation. He must do that soon before Reshmi begins to think he was the director general of police. "We'll make one for you on your next assignment, eh, Becka?"

"Yes, I'll take her measurements. I could do with an assistant."

Reshmi won't sleep tonight, Jasmine thought. The excitement of taking her father on would send adrenalin pumping into Reshmi's veins. Jasmine must warn her, though. Sunil would be even more dangerous this time. Having lost Jasmine and his family, he would draw blood. They had to be cautious about their entry and exit.

"Why don't you and your daughters stay with me tonight, Mrs Chari?" Rebecca said in casual tones, her cheeks turning pink as they looked at her.

Jasmine averted her gaze. She was damned if she would agree. She wanted to sleep in the safety and security of the officer's home.

Sid looked at Jasmine, waiting for her to speak up, but when she remained silent and Reshmi hesitant, he said, "Not tonight, Becka. They're kind of tired. So am I. Come, I'll walk you to the door."

Rebecca felt dismissed. A strange woman was going to share the roof with Sid—and probably his bed, while Rebecca, who worked at his side, wanting him, loving him...

Sid took the keys to the Audi and opened the door for her. Rebecca's heart thumped as they came close, Sid's freshly washed body emanating a fragrance of lemon and his potent aroma. When he leaned down and brushed a chaste kiss on her cheek, she turned her head and captured his lips. His body turned still, neither rejecting nor encouraging her as she pressed against him. Her arms wound around his waist as her mouth opened wide, begging him to give her what he'd been generously giving Mrs Chari. When she plunged a hand inside his robe and caressed his moist skin, he covered it with gentle pressure and stopped it from sliding dangerously close to his groin. He gave her a stern glance.

"I don't want to hurt you, Becka, but if you repeat this, I'll sack you. Do you understand?"

Rebecca combed a trembling hand through her hair. "You won't. I'm too good at my job," she said in a shaken voice. From the corner of her eye, she noted a movement at the French window overlooking the car park and knew that somebody had watched them—hopefully, it was Mrs Chari. Rebecca felt happy inside; she had conveyed the message. Sid was hers.

"Don't push your luck, Becka, you're not indispensable. See you tomorrow," Sid said abruptly. He turned on his heel and strode away without a backward glance.

Rebecca fired the engine, a sly smile on her face, not in the least put off by Sid's attitude. He would thaw with time, and she didn't mind waiting. He was worth waiting for. Moreover, Rebecca was working on a secret mission that would elevate her in his eyes, and then she would win him over.

CHAPTER SEVEN

Jasmine didn't raise her head as she heard the soft click of the automatic doors closing behind Sid. Hunched over a second cup of tea, she stared unseeingly towards the garden. Of course, it was silly to feel so emotional by what she had seen, but she couldn't deny how she felt. She wished she hadn't fallen prey to her curiosity. Reshmi had gone to the window to call out to Sid when she realised he was taking a while to return. Hearing Reshmi gasp, Jasmine hurried to her side, thinking the worst, as usual—that Sunil had somehow caught up with them. She had watched with dismay how Sid and Rebecca had kissed and embraced.

Her cheeks were aflame with embarrassment, and she felt they would betray her further. She had to remind herself of the reality of the situation. This was Sid's house, his domain, and any relationship he and Rebecca shared was his business. Jasmine and her children were only guests for a night. She mustn't forget that. She mustn't read too much into the dynamics of the household.

"Why aren't you in bed?" Sid asked with a frown as he advanced towards the bar, where Jasmine sat on one of the bar stools, cradling her cup.

Jasmine hesitated to meet Sid's gaze directly, her eyes darting to the side. "Um, should I make you some dinner?" She wished Sid would stop scrutinising her with those warm, chocolate-fudge eyes and that half-smile playing on his lips. Why was he smiling? Had he somehow sensed her watching them earlier?

Barely waiting for his nod, Jasmine slid off the stool and hurried to the kitchen. Inspecting the variety of vegetables he stocked in his double-door Siemens refrigerator, she selected a few ripe tomatoes, two vibrant green chillies, brinjals, a fresh bunch of coriander, and a bottle of ginger and garlic paste. From a small basket, she took a medium-sized onion, a sprig of fragrant curry leaves, and some fennel seeds. She boiled a few eggs, grated a portion of coconut, strained a cup of milk from it, and cooked a batch of Lal Qilla Basmati rice. Finally, she placed an induction tava on the electric hob, found the bottle of oil, and added mustard seeds and other ingredients to the tava.

As she worked, a series of thoughts swirled in Jasmine's mind. Did Rebecca do the shopping for him? Did they spend a lot of time together? And why should that matter to her? He was single, attractive, and could do anything he wanted.

Sid followed Jasmine to the kitchen, holding a glass of wine for himself and her unfinished cup of tea. He took a stool, fascinated with the image of having a woman in his kitchen. Not any woman. Jasmine Chari. Dressed in a soft-cotton baby-pink salwar kameez with a transparent pink chunni tied around her neck, she seemed to fit the role. The bruises on her face were barely noticeable; she must have concealed them, her experience of being regularly assaulted making her an expert with the make-up brush. Her hair was braided so that it didn't come in her way as she cooked, and he could see that she was far away in thought.

Sid's eyes pursued her as she moved from the sink to the stove to the wooden plank, chopping vegetables, boiling eggs, and crushing a range of eye-watering ingredients. He picked a tissue and mopped his eyes as they started to tear.

When she began to stir the paste and throw in some curry powders of different colours, the aroma permeated the air and took him back in time to the days his mother used to make him those once-in-a-day meals. He would sit on the cold mud floor and watch her prepare those appetising meals. Nothing fancy, just rice and egg curry, as that was all they could afford with the little money his father gave them. But his mother made sure she cooked the best egg curry ever. She would feed Sid until his tummy was full, and only then would she eat. Sometimes, he would pretend he'd had his fill so that she would have something left for herself. His eyes glistened, and he sponged them. Would he ever find her?

Jasmine turned to pick up the salt jar and saw Sid with such a forlorn expression that she became concerned. His broad shoulders were stooped, his hands were cupping his jaw, and she could swear he'd just wiped his eyes as the tissues were rolled in a ball.

Were those tears the effect of the ingredients, or was he crying? She knew he had cried in the car along with her children since Reshmi had mentioned it. She also said that he had suffered some kind of loss, perhaps identical to theirs, and helping them was making him feel better. Jasmine hadn't asked her daughter how she knew that as Reshmi had proved through the years that her intuitive abilities could be trusted.

With the fragrant curry simmering on the stove, Jasmine added grated coconut milk to the mixture and lowered the heat, allowing the flavours to meld. Her attention was now focused on Sid, who appeared increasingly vulnerable. Now her motherly instincts were clamouring to comfort him.

"If you prefer some other dish, I can make it for you," she said, halting by his side, her hands longing to touch his hair. "I thought an egg curry would be the quickest, considering the late hour."

He struggled to speak, the hard lump in his throat making it painful to swallow. He shook his head, hoping she would understand that it was not her curry that made him cry. She reminded him of the past. He knew these visits to his childhood days were ruining his present, but he couldn't help himself. Every time he achieved something, he wished his mother were there to see what had become of her son.

When was he going to find his mother? Would he ever see her?

"Sid?" Jasmine whispered, using his name for the first time. She was certainly worried as all through the day she had addressed him as 'officer' or 'Mr Chevalier'.

"It is fine, Jasmine. I like egg curry. Always did."

She breathed in relief and stirred the gravy after adding tamarind water to it. The same recipe as his mother, but coming to think of it, Jasmine was originally from Pondicherry, so wasn't it natural she would cook in the same style as his mom?

Jasmine heaped his plate with steamed rice, thick gravy, two eggs, and a dish of seasoned lady's-finger. She even fried some *appalams*. Then she hunted in the cupboards, searching no doubt for a bottle of pickle. She pulled out all the bottles that Sid had in stock, from spicy mango and lemon to prawn and fish.

Sid looked up at her and gave a wide smile, deeply appreciative that she had cooked him a meal despite her exhausting day. "Thank you." He didn't wait another minute. He couldn't. All those aromas had turned him ravenous for a home-cooked meal.

Jasmine could see that Sid was hungry as the fork and knife worked very fast. She dragged a chair and sat down and watched him eat. There was a faint flush on his face as he forced himself to pause for the sake of good manners. She smiled in mild amusement as he asked in between mouthfuls, "Aren't you having anything?"

Her lips widened, and her teeth flashed for a minute, and she realised with a start that it was her first smile.

"I had a sandwich earlier," she said. But the truth was she couldn't eat a thing. Even Reshmi refused a snack, saying the burger was sufficient.

His gaze met hers. "You're a good cook, Jess. I will employ you full-time."

The smile he shot Jasmine told her that, as far as he was concerned, she did everything well. She couldn't deny the pleasure she felt at the thought.

Outside, there was a cat mewing. She had been there for a while, eyeing Jasmine with that green, unblinking stare all through her activity as if she were keeping tabs on her. Undoubtedly, Sid fed her as she looked very well nourished.

Jasmine rose and came to stand beside Sid, a habit she had acquired from looking after the male folk—first her father and then Sunil. However, they never showed appreciation or acknowledged her presence. But Sid was different. He made Jasmine feel worthy right from the time their eyes met.

If only...

Sid smiled at her. She smiled back.

"Another helping?" she asked.

He shook a finger at her and said with a teasing grin, "You're set to fatten me up?" His eyes were like melted chocolate as they rested on Jasmine, making her blush as they told her secrets, secrets of what he wanted to do with her.

Was she imagining this? Was Sid telling her that he found her attractive? Jasmine had never considered herself pretty and hadn't given her looks much thought. And then she had Reshmi and Mira, and there was no time for anything else. But if she was honest, she would admit that she had been afraid Sunil would suspect her of having a lover if she took care of herself.

"You can afford it," she murmured, deliberating on those painful memories of her husband. It was easy for her to get carried away with the romance developing between the officer and her. But at the back of her mind, there was a gnawing thought that Sid was young, rich, and attractive. Why would he want to be saddled with a married woman with children?

"So, I'm thin?" Sid asked, interrupting her thoughts.

"You know you're not."

"Look at me, Jess." He caught her shy gaze and held it. "Do you know you are the first woman after my mother who has cooked me a meal?"

Jasmine hid her excitement and asked, "Doesn't Rebecca know how to cook?" She hoped to find at least one flaw in that woman. The worst part was that Jasmine was beginning to like her, and so was Reshmi. But after the latter had caught Rebecca with her favourite Uncle Sid, who she'd decided would suit her mother better, her affection for Rebecca had diluted.

"You'll have to ask Becka," he said with a mischievous grin.

"Surely, she'd have stayed here sometime? I mean..." Jasmine's cheeks bloomed as Sid's lips curved into a wide smile.

Damn! Why did she have to be so inept? Couldn't she have learnt to be more sophisticated from all those years with Sunil?

Jasmine remembered how Sunil had pursued a young, beautiful Brazilian model at a party without the slightest concern for Jasmine's feelings. She later learned Sunil had struck lucky; the girl became his latest mistress. Sunil spent lavishly on her, setting her up in a luxurious apartment, paying her bills, and buying her a flashy Ferrari. Jasmine had discovered this by accident when she came across the company's balance sheet on Sunil's desk, and the liabilities section appeared substantial. Although Jasmine didn't understand much about finances, she had telephoned the company's chief accountant, her father's crony, Mr Krishamoorthy. Through gentle persuasion, he revealed quite a bit about her husband's glitzy lifestyle.

"Are you asking if Becka and I are together?" Sid's teasing tones drew Jasmine out of her dark thoughts. Jasmine shook her head. Sid was nothing like Sunil, yet she was reticent to get into a situation that would complicate matters.

"Not at all. It's your life. How could I get so personal?"

Sid didn't look away from her averted face that had turned bright red. "There's nothing wrong in feeling attracted, you know," he said.

"I'm not..." She paused, seeing the disbelief on his face. "Fine, I am. You are a handsome man. After what Sunil put me through, any gentleman would catch my attention."

"So, you didn't mind seeing Becka and me kiss?"

Jasmine's eyes darted away in embarrassment. How did he know? Surely, he couldn't have seen her from that distance? God! This was getting more and more awkward.

She forced herself to meet his laughing gaze, irritated that he was finding it amusing. "Why should I? You're a free man. You have your life, and I have mine."

"Good, so that's settled then," Sid said and stood, tired of the game. Let Jasmine deny the attraction, but he wasn't going to lie about his reaction. Jasmine was his cup of tea, complicated as she was. What's more, he adored her children. He knew the consequences of getting involved with a victim, and that too, the wife of a powerful man. Becka was right. He had to have his head examined.

Jasmine picked up the dirty plates and moved towards the sink as if the conversation had never happened.

"Leave it there. I'll put it in the dishwasher later," he said, peeved.

She paused, looking at his rigid face, and heaved in a long breath, letting it hiss slowly as she placed the plates in the sink. The air started to charge with tension as she came towards him, halting a foot away, the top of her head reaching his chest. "I lied."

From outside his window, Sid's stray companion, the green-eyed, sleek feline, glared at him. He hadn't given her the bowl of milk, and it was way past her dinnertime. She meowed.

"Seeing Rebecca in your arms unsettled me."

What temptation was this in the midst of a rescue operation? Should he take Jasmine in his arms and tell her how much he was attracted to her, or better still, show her? Even without her laying a hand on him, his body hardened, and the stir between his legs became so obvious that he was sure she must have noticed.

He reached out a hand to gently touch her cheek. "Becka and I are not romantically involved."

"So why kiss her then?"

He squatted on a stool and dragged Jasmine between his legs. Her arms encircled his neck, her fingers caressing his hair like how she'd do with Reshmi and Mira. Sid let his head drop against her chest, loving the feeling that was creeping over him as her breasts pillowed him.

Soft ambient light filtered through the window, casting a warm glow on their entwined figures. The air was filled with the delicate scent of jasmine, adding a touch of enchantment to the moment. In that tender embrace, their worries and uncertainties melted away. Their eyes met, and in that gaze, they found solace, understanding, and a spark of something deeper.

"I was consoling her, Jess. She's been in love with me for years. When I brought you and the kids home, she fell to pieces. I've never been the social kind. You understand?"

"I don't want to be in the way."

"Do you like being here, Jess?"

"I feel like I've come home."

His heart thumped with happiness. Jasmine was speaking his thoughts aloud. He, too, felt an affinity with her and her children. Was it any wonder that Becka had got her hands into his robe? She must have been afraid of what would happen with him clamouring for Jasmine.

He didn't want to think of the future. He didn't want to question his emotions or Jasmine's. For some reason, they had met. He believed it was the unseen hand that had got them together. Maybe his mother was working from wherever she was.

She cupped his jaw. "I don't want anything to happen to you, Sid. My husband is very influential. What if he destroys your agency?"

Sid covered her icy hand with his warm one. "Don't worry. It won't happen. Just promise you won't go running back at the first hurdle like you wanted to do a while ago."

"I only offered because I was worried about your phone."

"Becka will handle that. But we can't live together, Jess. It will hinder the case." He broke the embrace and stood, giving her a slight push in the direction of the corridor. "Go to bed, now."

Jasmine's footsteps echoed softly in the quiet corridor, muffled by the plush carpet beneath her feet. Her thoughts were a jumble of conflicting emotions. Sid's tenderness was so different from Sunil's cruelty.

With a sigh, she reached her room and leaned against the door, feeling the weight of her responsibilities settling upon her shoulders. She knew she had to push aside any thoughts of romantic entanglements, no matter how tempting they might be. Her priority was to rebuild her life to create a safe and stable environment for her children.

The room was spacious and designed for a bachelor, and the furniture was modern and not elaborate like in their penthouse. Her gaze flickered towards the French window, where the cream blinds created a serene backdrop against the outside world. Her eyes shifted from the bed, big enough to host Jasmine, her children, and Sid if she wanted.

A startled laugh escaped her lips, a mixture of amusement and self-reproach. What was she thinking? Was she seriously considering the idea of sharing a bed with Sid? It was a dangerous thought that could only lead to complications and further entanglements.

She checked on Reshmi and Mira in the adjoining room and found them fast asleep with their arms around each other. It was their first peaceful night. She closed the door, not wanting to disturb her sleeping daughters.

She undressed and entered the luxurious marble-tiled bathroom with shower stall, tub, and toilet, stepped under the shower, and let the warm spray cleanse her body. Sunil's groping hands had left marks all over her, and they still stung as she scrubbed her body. Jasmine always carried antiseptic cream with her. Years of Sunil's brutality had made her carry a first-aid and make-up kit with her.

A showcase window adorned with lush green plants offered a touch of nature. The rectangular mirrors with white storage units reflected her image, creating an illusion of spaciousness. Fluffy towels hung on handrails, and a beautiful floor rug under her feet added a touch of warmth and comfort.

She headed to the mirrored wardrobe, which reflected her weary but determined gaze, and drew the crystal-handle door open. She browsed through the hangers, looking for a soft cotton shirt that would envelop her and leave some breathing space. Her large breasts had to be accommodated, and she picked an off-white, non-stretch shirt and sighed under the pleasant fabric. Closing the wardrobe, Jasmine made a mental note to ask Reshmi to gather their essentials and the money she had saved.

The shirt fell below her knees, and she folded the sleeves over her slim wrists right to her elbow. She didn't mind what she looked like as it was dark, and all she was going to do was sleep. She needed one night of peaceful slumber, too. Waiting up for Sunil had taken a toll on her health as she never knew in what state he would return. Sometimes, if she were lucky, he would only force himself on her without beating, biting, and scratching, but if he returned in a bad mood, there was no saying what the night would hold, like their last intercourse. Jasmine closed her eyes and found tears pushing through her clenched lids.

She crawled to the centre of the bed, which seemed to swallow her small form, and pulled the sheet over her head. She'd offered her daughters the option of sleeping in the same bed, but Reshmi said that she and Mira were comfortable in the guest room as they were used to having their own room.

There was a knock on the door just as she dozed off, and her heart fluttered as she wiped off her tears. She dragged herself from the bed and sleepwalked to the door, making a face at her reflection. What did it matter anyway? It wasn't as if she needed to look nice for him, did it?

The sight of Sid stirred a whirlwind of emotions within her, pulling her out of her haze of resignation. Sid was standing there looking apologetic as he pointed to the washroom.

"I need my razor and some other stuff," he said.

With a heavy sigh, she stepped aside to let him pass, her eyes lingering on his retreating figure. The fleeting connection they had shared, filled with warmth and tenderness, seemed to have evaporated at that moment, leaving her with a profound sense of disappointment and a tinge of sadness.

She must be dead on her feet for her to resort to building up images of the officer and her. What a laugh! She slid under the sheet once again and closed her eyes wearily, embarrassed by her romantic thoughts. The air conditioner was set at the right temperature, and it worked silently and efficiently, lulling her.

The room was in darkness except for a night lamp, and her lashes fluttered open drowsily when she felt the mattress dip. She saw a large shadow hovering over her. For a moment, she panicked and almost, screamed, reliving the nightmare. But the hand that caressed her forehead was gentle. Definitely not Sunil.

Her breath hitched in anticipation as she realised it was Sid. Her heart raced in her chest, pounding with excitement. The room seemed to grow warmer, the air thick with an electric tension, and her body tingled with desire.

"Did I scare you?" he asked, his warm lips brushing the curve of her cheek, burning a trail to her lips. "I wanted to say good night."

His bare chest pressed over her, and her heart started to

hammer savagely as she got a whiff of his cologne. Unlike with Sunil, where fear was the primary emotion whenever he came to her side, here, she quivered in anticipation. Sid looked so male, so deliciously male, and was watching Jasmine as if he was waiting for her to say something, do something, so that they could prolong the moment.

"Are you sure you will be comfortable in the lounge?" Her question hung in the air, laced with vulnerability and uncertainty.

Jasmine wished she could have said something more sophisticated like Rebecca would have said. The blonde beauty would not have searched for words; she'd have invited Sid with poise to share her bed. But Jasmine had no experience in courtship; the only man in her life had been Sunil.

His eyes were fixed on hers as if he knew the turmoil in her mind and was trying to read between the lines.

"Are you offering to share yours? His lips stroked back and forth on hers, and she parted them to taste his flavour. This would probably be the last opportunity she got with the officer. God knew what waited for her in the future. Why shouldn't she spend one night in his arms and learn what it felt like to be loved?

He gave a deep groan as he pushed his tongue inside her mouth and made love to hers, showing her with lips, teeth, and tongue that pleasure was sweet. Love was mutual.

When Jasmine's arms crawled around Sid's neck and drew him closer, when she hungrily sought him, allowing his tongue to wander and play with hers, Sid knew he had succeeded in showing her that there was another side to love, a side her husband hadn't shown her.

He wasn't rough like Sunil as he slid his hands over her enormous breasts. Instead, he caressed them and unwrapped them with care. She arched in pleasure as he unbuttoned her shirt, pushed the edges away, and nuzzled her breasts. He touched, felt, and massaged, and she drew his head to her breast and let him suckle.

Sid was doing so with great enjoyment. He made relishing sounds as he concentrated on arousing her to the heights of passion. She groaned and thrashed as he transferred his mouth to the other, and she dragged him on the bed beside her and drew the sheet over their heads.

CHAPTER EIGHT

Jasmine came wide awake as she heard loud squeals carrying through the partially open door. She glanced at the bedside timepiece and sat up startled. It was 9.00 a.m. She rubbed her sleepy eyes and looked around the unfamiliar surroundings.

The sunlit room was too bright for her drowsy eyes; some enthusiastic devil had raised the blinds to wake her. The bedcover fell away, and she flushed when she realised that her shirt was open, her breasts visible. She covered her blazing cheeks as flashes of the previous night teased her senses. Sid had made such sweet love to her throughout the night, and they barely slept. She wouldn't call what they shared 'sex'. It was love. She knew the difference now. Nothing would make her feel guilty for spending one night of passion with Sid.

She took a deep breath, reminding herself that this was a temporary reprieve from their troubles.

There were no signs of Mira and Reshmi as Jasmine jumped out of bed, tripping over the bedcovers in haste, her face furiously bright as she suddenly thought of her daughters seeing her with Sid. She remembered how his hands had wandered inside her shirt and stayed there stubbornly, although she had tried to relocate them.

She quickly straightened her dishevelled shirt and smoothed her hair, hoping to regain composure. Her mind raced with conflicting emotions. On the one hand, she longed for the intimacy they had shared, the tenderness absent from her life for so long. On the other hand, the fear of how her daughters would react if they found out gnawed at her. She wanted to protect them from the complexities of adult relationships, shielding them from the harsh realities she had endured.

Would her children have seen them together? Damn! What if Mira had woken up and come to cuddle her mother like she often did in the past? Sometimes, Sunil had made a place for his daughter, and at other times, he'd send her right back with a stern warning not to disturb her parents.

Jasmine buttoned her shirt and made the bed, trying to put the thoughts of Sunil behind her. She was with Sid now, and he had proved that all men were not like her husband. She hadn't felt any pain as he penetrated her. Coming to think of it, she had risen halfway to meet his thrusts. What a pleasant surprise. Instead of hurting her, he had Jasmine fighting to have him completely buried inside her. Even after they had reached the peak and their bodies shook, trembled, and shattered, they remained joined together, their arms around each other.

Her breasts responded to her thoughts and turned hard against the fabric of the shirt, and she wished she could have had another tumble before reality set in. A loud squeal of excitement sent Jasmine scampering after her kids, her thoughts on what mischief they were up to. No wonder they were not around her. They must be turning the place upside down.

Why was Sid allowing them to get away with this bad behaviour? Granted, he loved to fool around with her children, and they adored him in return. But that didn't mean they should take advantage of him.

She followed the excited shrieks through the corridors, noting as she went the ultra-modern console with its silver vase overflowing with tulips and the beautiful modern paintings in their platinum-plated frames. She had to admit that Sid had good taste. His villa was a combination of luxury and elegance —just the right size for Jasmine and her daughters, her heart whispered.

She sent that thought out of her mind, knowing it would be foolish to wish for something she might never have. Yes, Sid was attracted to her as she was to him, but it wouldn't be fair to saddle him with responsibility. She placed her ear against the door from where she could hear laughter mingled with loud music. Taking a deep breath, she pushed the door open.

Her jaw dropped as she gaped in stunned disbelief. Sid was bare to the waist, sweat rolling off his smooth body, his track pants running low as he dipped and rose in a perfect pose, obviously exercising, while her daughters stood on his sleek back with their knees bent and arms outspread as if they were surfing. They hadn't seen Jasmine as yet as they were fully concentrated on keeping their balance. Sid had increased his pace, and they rocked dangerously, holding on to each other and refusing to topple.

The floor was sheathed in velvet carpet that would cushion their fall if they lost balance, but the way they were holding their position made Jasmine want to join them and see whether the strong man would be able to continue his push-ups.

"Hi, sleepyhead!" Sid called out to Jasmine, deliberately drawing her daughters' attention. They were momentarily distracted—no, dismayed, as they stared at Jasmine, aware that she was displeased, and Sid chose that moment to roll over and send them tumbling to the soft carpet.

Her daughters became indignant, forgetting their mother was witnessing their unruly behaviour. They pounced on Sid like two ferocious beasts and unleashed their playful fury on their newfound friend. Reshmi and Mira punched Sid, and he let himself get bullied as her children mauled him.

Mira caught him on the jaw with a fist while Reshmi climbed on him and held him down. They refused to budge until he apologised to them. He wore a wide grin, playing along and accepting their proclamation of victory with good-natured surrender.

Jasmine was about to interrupt when Sid wriggled free and leapt from the floor swiftly, making straight for Jasmine. Her heart thundered as his strong arm wrapped around her waist, holding her to him like a shield. She ignored the damp, rugged body with its potent male scent clamping her from behind, the hard pelvis thrusting into her womanly curves. He lifted her off her feet and blocked Reshmi and Mira's advances. With playful determination, they pursued Sid, their giggles and shouts filling the air. Jasmine's breath quickened as she locked eyes with Sid over her shoulder.

Jasmine didn't know whether to be angry with Sid or her daughters, but at the moment, it seemed like her daughters needed to be disciplined. She couldn't believe the things they were doing under Sid's roof. It was like he had given them free access to be their mischievous selves, the way he had given Jasmine free access to his body.

"Reshmi! Mira! That's enough. Go and have your bath."

"But, Mom!" Reshmi looked at Jasmine as if she was spoiling her fun.

Ignoring Sid's proximity that made her feel warm and lethargic, she glared at Reshmi. "I said, that's enough." She kept a stern face with great difficulty. Sid chose that moment to nuzzle her neck in the pretext of defending himself from her little horrors, and she struggled to stay serious.

Reshmi gave Sid a fierce glance as she passed him. "I'm not finished with you." Sid gave a mock shudder. Mira showed a fist at Sid, imitating her sister's scowl, and Sid had possibly made some funny faces at her as she ran out giggling.

Sid's arms loosened around Jasmine, and she slid out reluctantly, the shirt damply plastered to her back. He plucked a towel from the rail and began wiping the sweat off his body in swift strokes, ruffling his hair in the process.

Jasmine couldn't tear her eyes away as Sid's muscles flexed and glistened under the soft lighting of the room. Her gaze followed the droplets of sweat as they trailed down his toned chest, disappearing into the towel's embrace. There was a raw magnetism about him, a confident allure that drew her in despite her efforts to resist. The sight of him, so effortlessly masculine and unapologetically himself, stirred a longing within her that she had long suppressed. He not only looked very yummy, he smelled yummy, too.

When had she become such a glutton for physical beauty? Jasmine sighed, ashamed of her wanton behaviour but unable to take her eyes off him.

"Like what you see?"

Jasmine's eyes abruptly left his chest and rose to meet the warm gaze examining her with gentle enquiry. She turned away from that sensational body, wishing she didn't feel so light-headed when he was around. But the imprint of his tender hands as they explored her body the previous night was teasing her senses. He hadn't asked anything in return but had just held her against him, whispering that he didn't mind waiting until she was ready to be wholly and completely his. At that precise moment, Jasmine had decided to give herself to him.

"You know you look good," she said.

"That wasn't my question."

"Okay, you look deliciously male. Satisfied?"

"You don't sound happy about it."

She looked at the discontented face, feeling like she was dealing with another child. What did Sid want her to admit? He knew she was attracted to him. What more did she have to say to convince him?

"You're worse than Mira! Do you want me to cuddle you?"

He nodded without hesitation, his chocolate eyes blazing as he took her hands to his perfumed chest and left them there, encouraging her to touch him. He cupped her waist with his large hands and drew her close, allowing her to feel his hardness.

"Last night was wonderful, Jess. I slept like a baby."

"Me, too. Did Reshmi and Mira see us?"

Sid lowered his head and covered her lips with his, and her arms entwined around his waist. She didn't care that he was half-naked and she was still in his shirt. She didn't care her children could interrupt them at any time. She was engrossed in giving out her love in large doses as Sid drank from her lips.

"I left before they woke up," he said, planting a trail of kisses down her jawline.

"So, they found you in the gym?"

He nodded without meeting her gaze. Reshmi had shaken him awake and saved his butt before Mira had woken up and come in search of her mother. He had sleepwalked to the canapé in the hall and thrown himself on it. The little horrors had barely given him a few minutes of rest before they dragged him to the gym, where they demanded that he give them a free ride on his back.

"I'm having so much fun, Jess."

"You are good for us."

Sid's arms tightened around her waist, his mouth telling her what her words were doing to him. He wanted to lay her on the carpet and take her leisurely in broad daylight, but there was so much to do that he had to postpone the moments of pleasure.

The door swung open, and Reshmi stood there looking somewhat impatient to see them still in an embrace.

"Mom, Becka has come. Hurry up. And you—" she pointed to Sid sternly, "get dressed, or Becka will be mad. She's already asked where you slept last night!"

Sid and Jasmine looked at each other in discomfort and then at Reshmi. She was trying not to smile as she watched their guilty expressions. Of course, she knew they had slept in each other's arms, and she was fine with that. Her mother needed a real man, not a sadist like her father.

"Hell! What did you say?" Sid asked, more worried for Jasmine than himself. Becka was going to handle Sunil today and needed to have a peaceful attitude. Considering Becka had been trying to occupy the position of his woman for a while, he didn't want that to play against her better instincts.

Reshmi shrugged. "That you were in the lounge and Mom was in the bedroom. Did I get that wrong?"

Her tone was so innocent that Jasmine gave Reshmi a censorious glance. She had a feeling Reshmi knew and was secretly happy. She had always told Jasmine she should leave that maniacal husband and find a real man.

"Tell Becka we'll be with her in a minute. Now, get cracking." Sid grinned at Reshmi and winked. Reshmi winked back and rushed to convey the message.

Sid turned towards Jasmine with such a disgruntled expression that he looked adorable. Mumbling about early risers, he said, "I'll make us some breakfast." He kissed the protest off Jasmine's lips and then kissed her some more until she tore herself away with a breathless laugh. He chased her to the bedroom, threatening to come in if she wasn't ready in five minutes.

Jasmine was still smiling as she showered, wondering why, in all the years she was married to Sunil, she had never felt this happy. She stared at her reflection and admired her heavy breasts for the first time. She had never liked them as they had attracted too much male attention. But last night, Sid had caressed them until they were ripe with desire.

Rebecca's husky laughter carried all the way to the bedroom. Jasmine hurried to the closet, inspecting the rows of shirts and debating on which one to steal. She found a pale pink one in natural silk that pasted itself to her damp skin. Her underwear barely covered her heavy breasts and shapely bottom. Sunil had always chosen sexy lingerie to enhance her already buxom figure.

As she caught a glimpse of herself in the mirror, she noticed the shirt reached below her knees. To accessorise it a bit, she chose a grey tie and belted it at the waist and shortened the length above her knees. She wore the same flip-flops in soft tan leather, and they seemed fashionable when matched with the outfit. There was no time to run a comb through her thick, knotted hair, so she wore it in a loose braid. The transformation was immediate. The soft pink shirt accentuated her warm complexion, and the loose braid added a touch of effortless charm to her appearance.

She must ask Reshmi to smuggle some clothes for her as she couldn't continue to wear Sid's shirts, particularly if they were going to live in an apartment by themselves. She skipped through the hallway, feeling young and attractive in her get-up, even more so when Sid wasn't able to look away. Her heartbeat accelerated as she caught the intensity of Sid's gaze, a silent invitation that seemed to tell her that if they didn't have an audience, he would have stripped the shirt off and taken her on that canapé.

What was happening to her? What were all these romantic thoughts she was harbouring? Shouldn't she be thinking of the difficult ordeal her daughter and Rebecca were about to face?

Rebecca choked on her greeting as she watched the man she loved look at Mrs Chari in a way he had never looked at Rebecca. But what made her gasp aloud was the shirt Mrs Chari was wearing. Rebecca had bought it for Sid's birthday. Her blood boiled as she thought of how they must have spent the previous night, and only Reshmi's innocent remark that Sid must have had an uncomfortable night on the canapé was a consolation.

"Shall we go?" Rebecca addressed Reshmi, avoiding Sid's dominating presence and Mrs Chari's radiant face. *Let them continue in their bliss for a little while more.* If there was one thing she knew about Sid, he kept his promises and threats. Last night, he had made it clear that he would sack Rebecca if she tried her stunts on him. Rebecca knew how she was going to get her boss to fall in love with her. She had a secret mission and was certain it would raise her in Sid's eyes soon.

Reshmi kissed her mother's cheek, a wide smile on her face. "Is there anything you want me to bring you?" She gave the outfit her mother was wearing a keen glance, her cheeks dimpling with mischief. "Some clothes, perhaps? Not that you don't look great in that shirt, Mom. You look hot. Doesn't she, Mira?"

Jasmine blushed at Reshmi's teasing remark. Gently patting Reshmi's cheek, she replied with a playful smile, "It would be nice to have some proper clothes. Also, there's some money hidden in my armoire between the folded clothes."

Mira nodded happily, repeating after her sister, "Mommy looks hot."

Sid scooped Mira from the floor and sat her on his broad shoulders as he walked Rebecca and Reshmi to the door. Jasmine followed behind, her heart thudding with anxiety as she saw Reshmi listening to the instructions. Jasmine knew her daughter was bright, agile, and quick and could outwit Sunil, but she felt callous for allowing Reshmi to accompany Rebecca into the lion's den.

Sid turned to Rebecca. "You'll have to watch out. The man is sharp, Becka. Not the usual kind of menace we encounter." His lips grazed Rebecca's cheeks. "If it gets dangerous, exit. Don't risk it, okay?"

"I'll take care, boss. Don't worry." Her voice was muffled as she was fighting the urge to kiss Sid again like she had done last night. Rebecca knew the risk involved with this case. If Sunil treated his wife in that way, what would he do to Rebecca if she was caught? But she wasn't afraid. She could take him on. For goodness' sake. She'd taken on thugs, bandits, and whatnot, single-handed.

Sid scuffed Reshmi under the chin, a tender smile curving

his lips. "Let Becka handle it, okay? Stay near the exit. Obey instructions. Don't do anything on the spur of the moment unless Becka calls for it. You will be safe with her."

Reshmi nodded and stepped away, meeting his glance. "Take care of Mom and Mira."

Sid leaned forward and kissed Reshmi's forehead, reassuring her he was there now and her burden was lightened. He would take care of them all. Reshmi must take care of herself now; she had lost enough of her childhood solving her parents' problems.

Sid forgot he had Mira perched on his shoulders as he leaned forward to kiss Reshmi's forehead. Mira shrieked as she tilted, too, her fingers grabbing Sid's hair.

"Mira falling down!"

Sid straightened, holding on to the child's ankles, reassuring her that he was a safe mode of transport. Kicking the door shut after Becka and Reshmi left, he slung an arm around Jasmine's shoulders, and they strolled towards the bar, where he slid Mira onto a tall bar stool and continued towards the kitchen. He would have normally used the table in the kitchen to have his breakfast, but he thought it would be fun for the child to pirouette on the bar stool whenever she liked.

He must discuss Rehmi's enrolment in school with Jasmine. He already had a meticulously vetted list of schools in their database. His agency, of course, would foot the bill, and later, through a lawyer, get Sunil's financial assistance for his children, if not for Jasmine. Not that it worried him if Sunil refused. Sid would make it his primary duty to see that Jasmine and her children were taken care of.

The familiar aroma of coffee filled the air as he expertly prepared a fresh pot. The clinking of cups and saucers echoed as he retrieved them from the cupboard, arranging them on a tray.

Jasmine watched him with admiration as he effortlessly navigated the kitchen, his muscles flexing under his unbuttoned body shirt. Sid turned towards her, catching her gaze, and a playful smile tugged at the corner of his lips.

"Eggs, bacon, toast, coming up," he said as poured the steaming coffee into the cups, the rich aroma enveloping the room. As he handed Jasmine a cup, their fingers brushed briefly, sending a jolt of electricity through Jasmine's body. She took a sip, the warmth of the coffee spreading through her, both inside and out.

Mira was swinging her little legs back and forth on the stool. "Mira wants milk," she commanded.

Sid came out with an apron around his neck and a tray in his hands and winked at Jasmine as he bowed before Mira and said respectfully, "One glass of milk for Ms Chari."

Jasmine contemplated the handsome chef who had pulled on a body shirt, probably in haste, for he had left it unbuttoned, and all that tanned skin beneath was sending her pressure skyrocketing. He was still wearing the same track pants low on his hips, and seeing him in the kitchen made her dream of many more meals together.

Mira glowed under his attention and said with her chin upthrust, "Mira wants orange juice."

Sid darted to the kitchen, keeping up the waiter's act, much to her daughter's delight, and came running out with a glass of fresh juice. He placed it on the countertop. "Orange juice for Ms Mira."

When the chubby hand rose once again, Jasmine pulled it down before her daughter sent Sid back to the kitchen for something else. Her children were definitely going overboard. They had never been this naughty.

Sid expertly whipped up eggs and bacon, whistling a popular song as he added sausages and chopped mushrooms and tomatoes. He moved around the kitchen, handling the ingredients like he was born to cook.

A smile played on Jasmine's lips as she said, "You're quite a chef."

Sid grinned, flipping the eggs in the pan with a flick of his wrist. "I dabble in cooking occasionally," he replied over his shoulder. "It's a good way to relax and unwind."

As the aroma of the sizzling bacon filled the air, Jasmine was drawn in by the delicious smell. "Is that for us?"

He grinned. "You bet." He emptied the contents into a plate and headed in Jasmine's direction. Even before he reached her side, she shook her head and continued to shake it, but he placed it under her nose.

"I'm not a breakfast person," she said.

He dragged a stool close to Jasmine, pretending not to hear her protest. He didn't order her to eat. He didn't need to. His expression said he wasn't going to leave her in peace until she did.

Mira drew Sid's attention to her plate, insisting he saw how well she ate without any help. Sid watched her with an approving smile and praised her. He then slanted towards Jasmine and whispered, "You didn't eat anything from yesterday, Jess. If you continue like this, you won't have the strength to fight."

She forked a strip of fatless back bacon into her mouth, feeling guilty that Sid had gone through all that trouble to prepare it for her. He dug into a cocktail sausage, fed it to her, and waited patiently until she ate it.

"I hope we hear from them soon," she said, giving him a sideways glance as she sipped the glass of orange juice and dabbed her mouth with a tissue. "Sunil hates Reshmi, you know. If he gets hold of her, there's no telling what he'll do."

"He would have to be very strong to overpower Becka. She's a black belt, you know. Almost knocked me down!"

Jasmine couldn't imagine that happening; however, she wasn't going to contradict him. She had enough worries as it was. The admiration in his voice, however, couldn't be ignored.

"You admire her very much, don't you?"

There was no malice in her observation; it was just a statement. But he seemed to read between the lines for he didn't answer immediately; instead, he was examining her at close range, trying to guess where she was going.

It could be Jasmine's guilty feelings coming in the way, making her ponder over her actions. If she hadn't distracted Sid, he might have responded to Rebecca's obvious attempts to get him. Whatever! But Jasmine was human, too, and having Sid with her, even for a short while, showed her how happy they could be together. She wanted to live in that dream a little longer.

Sid's eyes rested on Jasmine's face, noting the worry lines marking her forehead, and he let his breath out in a sigh. "Why are you doing this, Jess?"

"She loves you."

"I don't feel the same way about her. I explained it all yesterday."

"If we hadn't met, maybe you…"

"Wrong! I like complicated women." He was smiling as he said that, and she felt his eyes running over her luscious curves with a kind of thoroughness that made her blush.

Mira sang to herself, porridge spattered over her face, dress, and countertop. But Sid didn't reprimand the child; instead, he took a bunch of tissues, wiped her face, and taught her how to eat without spilling. When she grasped the basics, he competed with her, and in the process, she ate the rest of her porridge without creating too much of a mess. She then started on the orange juice.

Leaving Mira to her orange juice, he turned his attention back to Jasmine with a perplexed frown. "Do you want me to fall in love with Becka?"

"No!" she retorted ferociously and looked away with blooming cheeks. He chuckled, and she shut her eyes, refusing to meet his laughing gaze.

"Why not?" he asked in a lazy drawl. "You were, after all, campaigning for her."

"Don't make me spell it out."

He turned her bar stool to face him and forced her to look at him. "I want to hear you say it, Jess."

She couldn't lie anymore. Her heart was bursting with love. She wanted his tender lovemaking every night, not just for one night, but she knew that it was wrong to feel such desire for him when he had his life to live and she had her problems to solve.

"Last night was one of my happiest nights, Sid. I felt at peace. Even on my honeymoon, I wasn't cherished in the way you cherished me."

"A little more of that, and I'll smuggle you to my bedroom again," he warned, keeping an eye on Mira. She had climbed down the stool and was now sprawled on the carpet in the lounge, watching the cartoon network he had switched on for her earlier.

"What if Sunil comes after us?"

"You'll be safe with me, Jess," he said, kissing her gently on the mouth and prolonging it. "There are alarms and cameras around the place. Gated security scrutinises visitors. I also left a word with Mashraf, the head of security. He will not let strangers inside."

She wound her arms around his neck and soaked up his strength, wishing he didn't have to go to work. But she knew he had to. There was so much to do, starting with the files on Reshmi's mobile. They had to be transferred to their lawyer. Then, the famous bond needed to be stolen from Sunil's safe. Reshmi knew the code, and hopefully, would remember to get it. Jasmine had never considered stealing the bond as she always felt that she would be unable to leave Sunil. Losing custody of her children and being left on the road with nothing had been her topmost worries—until now.

"I have to get ready for work. You're sure you'll be okay?" Sid asked with a frown.

Her eyes darted to his, her breath turning unsteady, the thought of being on her own petrifying her. She didn't want him to feel obliged to protect them 24/7, but she couldn't hold back her shivers, imagining the worst.

"Do you want me to stay with you?" His voice softened. He was willing to do anything to eliminate her fears.

"No, we can manage. Reshmi should be home soon, right?"

He kissed the tip of her nose, "Yes. If I know Becka, she won't take long to solve the issue. Reshmi will be back safe."

The whole day lay empty in front of Jasmine, but again, she was used to it as living with Sunil had left her many empty days. But the difference was that she wanted Sid to stay, whereas she'd never wanted Sunil around. How easily Sid had inserted himself in their lives.

Mira gave a loud wail as she saw Sid disappear down the corridor. In her mind, it meant bad Appa was coming back to take Mira and her mother. Sid retraced his steps, scooped Mira from the carpeted floor, placed her on his shoulders, and galloped down the corridor towards the guest room. Her wails turned into giggles as she bounced on his shoulders. Jasmine was galloping beside them as if she were racing with him.

He tumbled Mira on the bed, escaped to the washroom, and locked it from inside. Mira leapt and banged on the door, demanding he come out and play with her. Jasmine picked up her indignant daughter and left the room as the shower began to run. Images of Sid naked under the spray overwhelmed her, and she darted out of the room and shut the door behind them along with the images.

CHAPTER NINE

Residency Towers

Rebecca flashed her British passport, citing Mrs Arora's name as the person she was meeting. The plan had been carefully coordinated, and they had already informed Mrs Arora and told her not to deny it. With her identity established, Rebecca stepped on the accelerator of her sleek Audi, and they sped down the beautifully landscaped driveway. She had lent Reshmi a pair of stylish sunglasses that she had eagerly donned, a cap and a jacket, which the young girl wore with pride, insisting once again that she should have a uniform for the next operation.

They came in through the front gate as Mrs Arora buzzed it open. She informed Rebecca that Sunil was not around but to be vigilant in case the guards got suspicious. She wouldn't put it past Sunil to have informed security.

Rebecca's heart pounded in her chest as the eerie silence of the place set her nerves on edge. Her senses were heightened, and she remained alert for any sudden movements that might occur along the way. Beside her, Reshmi played her role of a subdued adolescent, sticking to Rebecca's side without a murmur of protest. They blended in effortlessly with a few residents and walked past the guards, who didn't give them a second glance. But Rebecca knew any moment could bring unforeseen challenges, and the mission required precision and stealth.

Afraid of being recognised, Reshmi suggested they use the

service lift. Though Rebecca would have preferred to take the stairs, she nodded and ducked into the lift. Just as the doors were about to shut, a security guard entered. He was surprised to see them there and enquired if they were employees. Rebecca was about to respond in Hindi, a language she managed well, when Reshmi interrupted.

"*Apna kaam dekho*! (Mind your business)."

Rebecca understood they were in trouble when the guard took a closer look at Reshmi and pulled out his walkie-talkie. Without hesitation, Rebecca flattened him with a sharp jab of her elbow and a kick in his groin. She grabbed Reshmi, and they made a run for the back door.

Reaching the back door, they slipped into the shadows, their breathing heavy and their eyes alert for any signs of pursuit. Despite Rebecca's instructions to make for the exit, Reshmi ran towards the gym, leading them straight into the lion's den. Perhaps she didn't hear Rebecca. Whatever! She continued her wild dash, and Rebecca had to make a split decision as she spotted several heavily built guards waiting for them in the gym.

Rebecca eyed her opponents, trying to see through their tough stance. There were sure to be weaknesses somewhere, she told herself. With a graceful and fluid motion, Rebecca struck, kicked, and blocked, years of training coming to her aid and bringing a certain flexibility that allowed her to shift effortlessly from one position to another. Her loose slacks and body shirt were her most comfortable gear, and she wasted no time. With lightning-fast reflexes, she anticipated the opponents' next moves and swiftly counter-attacked. She was breathing deeply and rhythmically, staying focused all through the fight.

Rebecca sprung on one man as he grabbed Reshmi and dodged a punch while Reshmi picked a light dumb-bell and swung it at the guard. Fired with adrenaline when she heard his howl, she flung whatever she found in the room randomly, and there was a lot of equipment.

Rebecca intensified her dodge-and-parry moves, staying one step ahead of her adversaries; however, her hair had come loose and got in the way, making it difficult to see through the tresses. One guard managed to grasp a handful of hair, and as Rebecca yelled, he punched her in the face. Hearing her cry, Reshmi crawled between his legs and bounced the dumb-bell on his groin. He screamed in agony, releasing Rebecca's hair and nursing his groin.

"Run, Reshmi. I'll handle them." Rebecca panted between kicks and blows. "Ask Sid to arrange reinforcement." But as Reshmi was about to escape, one guard grabbed her and hoisted her in the air. Reshmi screamed, kicked, and punched, but he was too strong for her.

Reshmi's heart pounded as the security guard carried her against her will, tears of anger welling in her eyes. She struggled in his grasp, but his grip only tightened, leaving her helpless and trapped. The elevator doors closed with a soft chime, and Reshmi's heart sank as she saw him press the button for the eighth floor. Dread washed over her as she realised they were heading straight to the Chari residence.

As the elevator doors opened on the eighth floor, her eyes met Sunil's sinister smile. He stood there exuding false warmth, his intentions masked behind a façade of charm. Sunil slipped a thick bunch of notes into the security guard's pocket with a devious smile, drew Reshmi inside, and shut the door.

The penthouse triggered a rush of painful memories for Reshmi. The opulence and grandeur that had once seemed impressive now felt suffocating, reminding her of her mother's years under Sunil's cruelty. Her anger towards Sunil simmered beneath the surface, making it hard for her to sympathise with the limping man before her. His gait was slow, and Reshmi couldn't help but notice the irony of his current condition. He deserved what he got for all the years he'd tortured his wife, yet she knew that revenge would not heal the scars he had inflicted upon her family.

Her primary concern was finding a way to contact Sid and get help. Rebecca was in danger. Reshmi's eyes flickered to the phone hanging on the lampstand, a glimmer of hope amid this nightmarish situation. She knew she had to act quickly before Sunil discovered the mobile or any hint of her plan. She had to be discreet, cunning, and swift. Every second counted, and she felt the weight of responsibility on her shoulders.

Sunil smiled. "You dared to enter Residency Towers with that European kung fu woman!" He barely gave Reshmi time to sit before he pounced on her, pushing his face close to hers. "Fortunately, I had tightened the security around the place after the last fiasco."

"Please, let Becka go. I beg of you. They are killing her."

He ground his teeth. "That police officer—my wife's lover, did you see what he did to me? I'll make him pay."

"Pop," she addressed him through gritted teeth, trying to maintain a semblance of composure despite her loathing for the man. But if she was going to save Rebecca, she could not antagonise him. "It is not her fault. She accompanied me. I wanted to see you."

"Really? You forget I know you, my dear girl. I'm the last person you'd want to see. But I'll get to the bottom of this, I promise."

Reshmi took a deep breath, trying to suppress her concern. Rebecca would come out of it; she had fought like an ace with a dozen men. The question that plagued her was how to inform Sid. Surely, he must be worried that they had not returned. Would her mother and Mira be safe?

"I need to call Mom," she said. "Please give me your phone."

"Not to worry, my dear, she'll be here soon."

Reshmi looked at him, panic-stricken. "Pop, don't frighten them. Mira is barely five. It will affect her. Bad enough she wakes up crying."

"Don't tell me how to handle the family, Reshmi. Your mother might have given you much attention but not me. I don't need your advice."

Reshmi contemplated her enraged father in silence. Why couldn't she have listened to Rebecca and made it to the exit? Not only did she bring suspicion upon them by telling that guard to shut up, but she also ran into a trap and dragged Rebecca along.

"I didn't mean to cause any trouble, Pop," she said, choosing her words carefully. She hoped her feigned vulnerability would distract Sunil from her earlier defiance and keep him focused on her.

"You attacked quite a few guards yourself. What were you trying to prove? I have to foot their hospital bills and compensate them generously."

Reshmi took a deep breath, maintaining a neutral expression under her father's scrutiny. "I didn't want to prove anything, Pop," she replied steadily. "I was just trying to protect Becka. I couldn't stand by and do nothing. She was in danger."

Sunil's eyes still held suspicion despite her sincere and remorseful face. "You always had a rebellious streak," he said, shaking his head. "Give me that officer's address."

Reshmi forced herself to meet her father's eyes. "I thought you said you said Mom would be here soon? Were you bluffing?"

Sunil smiled as his mobile buzzed, placing the call on speaker. Reshmi's face paled as she heard her mother and sister's hysterical cries. She leapt to her feet and advanced towards her father with a murderous expression.

"If you do anything to them, I'll kill you."

"Sit down! I'll tell them to hurt your mother otherwise. Did you think I wouldn't find them? You must know your father better than that."

Reshmi squeezed her eyes shut, blaming herself for the

situation. Sid had warned her to follow Rebecca's instructions, but Reshmi was so used to making decisions in the past that she allowed her instincts to rule. She'd underestimated the shrewdness of her father.

Her eyes stung with tears as guilt overwhelmed her. The gym normally had a few residents working out, and she had been counting on extra help. How could she have known that Sunil would have installed guards over there? Reshmi feared to think of Becka's state and felt helpless. She knew her father's capacity for brutality, and the mere thought of him instructing harm on Rebecca sent chills down her spine.

"Break everything in the villa," Sunil said to his men over the receiver. "Every goddam thing."

Warm tears gushed from Reshmi's tightly clenched lids. Poor Sid! What a repayment for having helped them. She watched wretchedly as her father glanced at his mobile when it pinged. He whistled through his teeth.

"Hmmm, Jessy looks very provocative in that man's shirt. She never looked this hot for me. Did she sleep with him?"

Reshmi cursed the colour that seeped under her skin. She hadn't prepared for this cross-questioning as the excitement of being with Rebecca and outwitting her father had preoccupied her. But she had some idea of how gorgeous her mother looked in Sid's shirt, standing beside him. There had been something in Sid's eyes when he had looked at her mother, and Reshmi knew it was not lust. She had seen lust on her father's face. But on Sid's face, there was love and tenderness.

What was going to happen to them now? Would her father expect his wife and children to live together with him as if nothing had happened? Reshmi shut her eyes briefly. She would not let that misfortune befall her mother. It would never be the same for her. Reshmi knew her mother had found something with Sid. She knew her mother very well. She wouldn't survive with Sunil—not after Sid's gentleness. In the past, when Reshmi had talked to her about leaving Sunil, they hadn't any idea that men like Sid existed. But now they had.

"You know Mom will never do that." Reshmi looked her father in the eye. "She loves you," she said with quiet conviction.

Sunil gave her a hard glance, trying to see through her story, but Reshmi maintained the expression, praying he would buy the lie.

"I never noticed. She only gave me pleasure when I forced myself on her. She didn't come to me otherwise."

"She was frightened of you, Pop. What did you expect?"

"She's mine. She and Mira are mine. You'll never see them again."

Reshmi bowed her head, knowing he could separate them. He had tried several times to send her to her maternal grandparents in France, but her mother had refused, threatening to leave if he insisted. It was only because of her mother that Reshmi had been allowed to stay. But now, all that was going to come to an end. Her father would make sure Reshmi left.

CHAPTER TEN

Sid replaced the receiver with a grim expression. He tried to clear his mind as he paced his bureau, inhaling and exhaling. He should have stayed with them. None of this would have happened. He would have fought until death to save them. He rubbed the sides of his head where it throbbed as he replayed what Mashraf had recounted. Poor Jasmine! How petrified she must have been. And little Mira, how she'd cried this morning when he was leaving the house. Had she sensed something?

"Any news of Becka?" Sid asked as he dropped into a chair.

"Yes, boss. Mrs Arora called. She found Becka in a sorry state. That man is a maniac. He got his men to beat her up until she bled. She was rushed to the hospital."

What kind of animals were these to bruise a woman in this way? And now, they had taken Jasmine and Mira by force. Sid should have anticipated Sunil's comeback. Sending a police officer with his men was a smart move. Security had to let them in, particularly as they explained that the woman and child were those of an influential businessman.

Sid should have trusted his instincts. Hadn't he been restless while he drove to the office? Hadn't he been tempted to return home and spend the day with Jasmine and Mira? They would have been safe in his care, and together, would have found a way to reach Reshmi.

Just the thought of Jasmine being dragged from the premises and thrown into the car made Sid feel violent. He looked at Roy hovering near his desk, undoubtedly preoccupied with Becka.

"Get DGP Blake on the phone. We need police backup. Inform the French Embassy that three French citizens are in grave danger."

Roy's face tightened as he watched his boss pace the office reception area. It was not the best moment to talk, but he hated to see him tense and unhappy. Sid didn't deserve this. For God's sake! Why was he risking his life for this woman? Becka was perfect for him. They had so much in common. Of course, Roy would have liked it if Becka had given him some attention, but she had never been interested in Roy except when Sid ignored her.

Why couldn't Sid fall for Becka instead of that complicated, troublesome character and her children? Becka had recounted to him every detail of the case, and the more she had said, the more worried Roy had gotten. Whatever had hit Sid when he was dealing with the Chari woman had hit him hard. He was not himself, and that was dangerous.

"Let them be, boss. You've done all you could. There's nothing more we can do. Why risk the reputation of our agency?"

Black rapier eyes flashed on Roy so fiercely that it made him shut up. Becka was right. Their boss was out of his mind where Mrs Chari was concerned. He was looking at Roy as if he wanted to murder him.

"Transfer the videos and photos from Reshmi's phone to Advocate Chowdary. Find a way to break into Residency Towers. We have never failed to rescue a woman because we are afraid… and never will."

Roy sighed resignedly as he returned to his desk and prepared the second rescue operation. His mind, however, was on Becka and how she was faring. Mrs Chari could go to hell for all he cared! Grinding his teeth, he picked up his phone and punched numbers.

The landline shrilled as Sid walked into his cabin, and Sid leaned over and grabbed it. He was expecting Sunil. The man was a psychopath, and with his family back there, he would wreak his revenge. The muscles at the back of his neck tensed, and he massaged it with one hand as he waited. He listened to the sounds in the background, trying to place where the call was coming from. He could hear the faint conversation in a language he hadn't heard in years but understood.

A choked sound emitted from Sid, his heavy body crashing into the chair as he held the phone to his ear. "Jess, is that you?"

A long, pain-filled breath released in a slow hiss.

Sid started to feel a strange sensation, as if he had heard that sigh before. Potent memories flooded, taking him back to his childhood, and he closed his eyes and let himself be swamped by recollections. He was lying on his mother's outstretched legs, and she was humming a Tamil song, 'Kannan Varuval, Kadhai Solluvan', as she rocked him to sleep. There were flowers in her hair, and her sari smelled of spices, and she was gently calling out to him, "Siddhu."

It took Sid a moment to realize the voice was real. His face drained of colour as he clutched the receiver to his ear. Only one person called him *Siddhu*, and he would recognise that voice even if he hadn't heard it in twenty-seven years.

"Amma?" It was *her*. He was certain. But how did she know where to call? How did she find him instead of him finding her? He was shaking so badly that the receiver was sliding from his grip. "Tell me I'm not dreaming."

She began to cry. Sid cried with her, the tension of the last hours taking its toll on him. His sobs were so deep that they wracked his body. He wept for the lost years, the times he felt alone and abandoned. The ache in his heart was still raw, and try as he did, he couldn't stop the flow of tears.

Roy wanted to rush towards Sid and put a comforting arm

around his shoulders but instead backed away, leaving him in privacy. He was proud of Becka, the trouble she'd gone through to do all the research in her leisure hours so that Sid would be reunited with his mother. Only recently had she confided in Roy, and Roy had advised her not to tell Sid until she was sure. Sid had had enough of disappointments in the past.

"Why did you leave me, Amma?" Sid had to ask her that. He needed to know. He was haunted by the thought that he had burdened his mother. Maybe he could now understand why she had avoided contact with his adoptive parents.

"I wanted you to have a good life, Siddhu... become someone. When the missionaries told me about a French couple wanting to adopt a child, I knew it answered my prayers. I had nothing to give you, Siddhu... only tears. I can close my eyes now and die in peace. I found my son."

"Where are you, Amma? I want to see you. I *need* to see you." Through the partition, he signalled Roy to book his ticket. Could Becka be behind this? Becka did tell Sid that she would leave no table unturned to find Sid's mother. She must have had something to do with this.

Roy made an online reservation for Sid on the first flight to Chennai, and from there, a chauffeured car to drive him to Pondicherry. As for Mrs Chari and her daughters, they could go to hell and stay there for all he cared. Roy had no intentions of following up on the case, although he reassured Sid he would stand in for him.

"Wait for me, Amma. I'll be there tomorrow," Sid said.

"Oh, my Siddhu. I never thought I'd live to see this day."

Sid hated disconnecting, but he had to leave now if he didn't want to miss the flight. Roy was buzzing him on the intercom. It looked like he had found a seat for him on Indigo Airlines.

"Take care, Amma. Save some hugs for me."

CHAPTER ELEVEN

The security guards walked Jasmine in her pink shirt through the reception area of Residency Towers. With Mira in her arms, Jasmine met the inquisitive eyes of a few gossipy aunties without flinching. Why should she? These men should be ashamed for breaking into Sid's villa and kidnapping her and Mira. Poor Sid! What a mess they made of his beautiful villa. She would make Sunil pay the damages.

The only positive side to this kidnapping was that she would see Reshmi. God knew how she was bearing up, and Jasmine was anxious about her. Mira had cried all through the journey, asking for her Uncle Sid and why he had not come like Superman to save them. Jasmine had reassured her that he would rescue them. He had promised them security, and he would keep his word. After that, Mira seemed less worried.

Mrs Arora came to greet Jasmine as the doors of the elevator opened. Jasmine gave her a sad smile, knowing she was probably wishing she hadn't interfered in Jasmine's life. But Jasmine was grateful that Mrs Arora had pressurised her to call rescue operations. She might never have met Sid and understood what it was to have a loving man at her side.

If only Jasmine hadn't opened the door this morning. Sid had warned her to be careful, but fool that she was, she had wanted to take the overflowing garbage bin outside. She had no idea that Sunil's men were hovering outdoors, although cameras were scanning the place, which was strange. Unless someone had disconnected the cameras and alarm system.

When Jasmine saw the men, she froze, and by the time

she got her act together, they had overpowered her. When Mira had seen them manhandling her mother, she had flung a cup of milk at one man and hit the other with a glass bowl. Jasmine had been so surprised that she giggled. Seeing her mother's approval, Mira bit a man's hand and kicked another man in the groin. Jasmine had looked on in amazement. Was Sid responsible for her daughter's sudden strength? Mira had become a warrior overnight.

Jasmine's eyes shifted to Sunil as he answered the door. He used support to walk, leaning heavily on it as he led Jasmine and Mira inside. Jasmine exhaled her suppressed breath. His aggression might have toned down, given his condition. At least, she hoped it was.

Mira chose that moment to wriggle out of her mother's arms and insist that Jasmine place her down. To Jasmine's astonishment, Mira tucked her tiny hand in hers, her expression as brave as Reshmi's would have been. On her face was a reassuring expression that she was there for Jasmine. Jasmine's eyes filled. She was indeed blessed to have her beautiful daughters looking out for her.

They followed Sunil into the dining room. The broken door hadn't been replaced yet. Sunil was probably going to use it as evidence against Sid. Jasmine would put nothing past her husband to take his revenge on Sid. A tiny part of her wondered what Sid was doing right then. He must have been informed about the kidnap. Mashraf would have told him. Could he be arranging a rescue?

The apartment resonated with silence Mira strolled towards the kitchen and looked around, probably for Reshmi. Not finding anyone there, she moved to the stock room, the lounge, and the study. Finally, she returned to the dining hall, climbed on a leather chair, and looked at her father. "Where is akka?" she asked.

Sunil looked at his favourite daughter, somewhat taken aback by her direct attack. So was Jasmine. Mira was not trembling and shuddering as in the past whenever she came in contact with her father. She was staring him in the eye without an ounce of fear.

"Do you want something to eat?" Sunil's eyes narrowed on her cherub face as she continued to stare him down. There was a tinge of disbelief and anger, which combined to give his face an unhealthy flush.

She shook her head. "Mira wants akka."

"She's in her room."

"You beat akka; Mira beat you," she said, climbing down from the chair. Then, asking Jasmine for permission to leave the room, she scooted down the corridor as fast as her little legs could carry her. The door opened and shut behind her.

Jasmine would have loved to run behind Mira and lock herself in with her children, but she was done with running. This man had to be faced, or he would continue to torture her for the years to come. She looked at Sunil and noted he was still in shock. Never had Mira addressed him in that way. He must be blaming Jasmine and her entourage for his daughter's behaviour.

"Did you sleep with him?"

Jasmine struggled not to blush and kept her expression bland. If Sunil suspected she had feelings for Sid, he would arrange to murder him and pass it off as an accident. He was capable of eliminating anything or anyone from getting in his way.

Bad enough they had damaged Sid's property and left his villa in a deplorable state; she would never forgive herself for bringing any more harm to him or his agency.

Sunlight filtered in through the silk drapes, turning the hall into an ominous shade of red. The white piano lay untouched. Reshmi and Mira had a music teacher who came in twice a week. Sunil's violence had made it difficult for Jasmine to interact with the teacher, so she avoided coming out of the room. The teacher had remarked to Reshmi that her mother seemed uninterested in her children's progress. Reshmi didn't want piano lessons after that, nor did Mira.

"You should know me better than that," she said, not meeting Sunil's gaze.

"You're wearing his shirt," he stated with cold contempt.

"I had nothing else to wear."

"If you hadn't left in such a hurry, you'd have thought of taking some clothes with you." His eyes dropped to her bare legs, heat kindled in those cruel, black depths.

Jasmine knew how she looked in the pink shirt. Apart from her hair that had come undone after that tussle with Sunil's bodyguards, the rest of her form was attractive. But the last thing she wanted was to draw Sunil's attention.

She shrank inside when his hand came to grab her breast and squeeze the nipple. Jasmine's eyes burned with angry tears. She hated his touch; he made her feel dirty. She couldn't let him have her after experiencing Sid's gentleness. If only she could flee into one of the rooms and lock herself inside. If only...

"He won't come for you this time, Jessy. He's busy nursing his assistant in the ICU."

"What kind of a man are you? How could you have hurt Rebecca?"

He stepped forward, his body grazing hers. "I told you not to play with me. You never listened."

Jasmine stepped back, her knees trembling. Sunil's hand kneaded her breast roughly. "That kung fu woman fought bravely. Looks like your officer trained her well." His hand shifted to the other breast, and he punched it playfully before his hand came out of the shirt. "Why is he even bothering with you when he has such a beauty at his side is beyond me."

Jasmine backed away, her steps unsteady as she noticed that Sunil wasn't limping anymore. The anticipation of forced sex seemed to have strengthened his limbs. The distance between Jasmine and the bedroom door was just a few steps away.

"He was only doing his duty. We called him for help," Jasmine said.

"Did you?" Sunil said in soft rage. "Well, this time, you won't have the strength to lift a phone." He lunged for Jasmine.

Jasmine dashed through the corridor, reached the master bedroom, and shut the door in Sunil's face, but her entire being was trembling as she tried to lock it from the inside. Sunil rattled the handle, pushed from the other side, and inserted a foot between the gap.

Crying with frustration, Jasmine moved back as Sunil shoved it with force, sending her sprawling backwards onto the mattress. Her shirt rolled up her thighs, her lacy underwear visible, while her breasts rose and fell, straining against the silky fabric.

Jasmine tried to tug the shirt down and cover her legs, looking around her desperately for something to defend herself. The golf clubs were in a bag at the corner of the room near the door, too far away from her reach. And Sunil advanced on her, seeming like he was in the mood for rough sex. A helpless scream built inside Jasmine as she saw Sunil's hands going to his zip.

"Don't do this, please. Let me go." She fought his grip, hitting and kicking at him, but he was too strong and grasped both her hands and held them above her head while he pulled down his trousers.

"Give me some of what you've been dishing out to the officer. I kept you like a queen for years, and all I get is this!" He gestured to her struggling beneath him, slapping her hard on the face. "After I'm done with you, no man will ever want you."

Jasmine fought him all the more, refusing to submit. She couldn't let him take her, not now, not ever. She didn't want this brutality. She wanted love... the sweet, tender love that Sid gave her. Where was he? Why hadn't he come for them? He must know by now that they'd been kidnapped. Was he having second thoughts after Rebecca was bruised? Could he have given up on them?

Her body sagged as her mind lingered on Sid and how peaceful it had been with him. Had she been alone, she'd have continued the fight with Sunil, but there were their children to consider. She should not anger him. Not now. Maybe after she got Reshmi and Mira safely out of his way, she could show him the other side of her. At least she hoped she had a stronger side to her.

As if thinking of her daughters made them appear before her, they were suddenly there by the door. Sunil had forgotten to lock the bedroom in his haste to rape her. Jasmine waved her children away before Sunil saw them. Their father was preoccupied. It was their best chance to flee. But Reshmi and Mira remained there, tears streaming down their cheeks. They seemed to say: *Not this time, Mom. We won't let him assault you again.*

Sunil thrust against Jasmine. "Missing the action, are you?" he said, enjoying Jasmine's agitated movements against him, unaware of the reason behind them. He tore the front of her shirt and seized her tethered breasts. "How I hungered for them," he grunted, placing sloppy kisses on the mounds and biting the nipples roughly. Jasmine's agonised scream halted midway as Sunil gave a startled cry and slumped on her.

Unable to move under the paralysing weight of Sunil, Jasmine looked at the collapsed form. Reshmi had the golf club in her hand, a smile of satisfaction on her face. Jasmine's eyes widened as Reshmi brought it down again on Sunil. Then she helped Jasmine heave the heavy weight off her body, and Jasmine fumbled with the buttons on the shirt, not wanting her daughter to see the bruises.

Reshmi placed her head on Jasmine's shoulders, and the

club dropped to the carpet. They cried with their arms wrapped around each other. Cried for the family they never had, cried for the man lying unconscious on the bed, and cried for the officer who hadn't come to rescue them.

Unnoticed was little Mira, who had climbed on the bed. She now had the club in her hand, bringing it down hard on Sunil's body. "Bad Appa!" she cried.

"Mira!" Jasmine called to the little fury standing on her father's body. Mira paused and looked at Jasmine. Jasmine held her arms open, and Mira let the club slide from her hand and slowly approached her mother and sister. Jasmine drew Mira into her arms and held her daughters against her thudding heart.

"Call Rescue Operations," she told Reshmi in hushed tones. "Stay with Mrs Arora until they arrive."

"No! We are not going anywhere without you," Reshmi whispered, eyeing her father's stirring form. "He will get up any time now and will once again hurt you. I'm not letting you go through this again."

Jasmine cried then, cried for the beautiful children God had given her, children who were sacrificing their safety for her.

"Do as I say. I'll be with you in a moment."

Sunil started to move, and Jasmine quickly bundled her children towards the door and pushed them outside gently. She picked up the discarded club and walked towards the closet that held the safe. She pulled on a kameez over her torn shirt and covered her bruised body.

It took her a few moments to find the money she had hidden between the folded garments. She emptied the contents into her handbag. Then she packed some necessities for her and her children as she didn't know when she would be able to retrieve their stuff. Sunil moved on the bed, and she sensed his hands reaching to grab her. Without hesitation, she turned and aimed the club at his head. His arms came out to shield his face as he screamed.

"Bitch!"

Jasmine tried the combination to the safe where the dreaded document was hidden. Her hands were shaking so much that she punched the wrong code twice. Taking a swift breath, she prayed silently and tried one last time. The safe unlocked. Jasmine picked up the document with revulsion, rolled it, and shoved it into her bag. She didn't want the company's investment certificates, property documents, jewels, and money. Let Sunil have them all. She just wanted peace of mind and custody of her children.

"Whore! Get out! Go to your lover. You'll never gain custody of Mira. You'll never breathe the same air as her," Sunil hissed.

"You can try. Mira won't come to you." Jasmine slung the bag over her shoulder and continued to the door. Turning the key, she looked over her shoulder, her deadly gaze pinning him, "I'm leaving you, Sunil. You follow me, I'll kill you."

"You don't mean that, Jessy. How would you run the family? On love?" He laughed harshly, his body shaking with mirth. "You've never lived a life of hardship. Every fucking thing was given to you on a platter—first by your father and then me."

"Don't worry. I'll figure out a way to look after my daughters," Jasmine assured with a determined tone.

"If you're depending on the officer, forget it. After I'm finished with him, he'll be on the road."

"And you'll be behind bars! We have videos of your violence, Sunil. It's over. Get that into your head. O.V.E.R."

Sunil made a loud noise and reached for his mobile. But Jasmine was there before him and knocked it out of his hand, sending it crashing to the floor. Then she trampled on it.

"I don't need you. I don't need any man to help me. See you in court."

Sunil's mocking laughter followed Jasmine as she stumbled out. She locked him inside and pocketed the keys. *Let him have a taste of helplessness.* By the time he got to the balcony and signalled someone, Jasmine and her daughters would be gone from there.

Reshmi and Mira were waiting for Jasmine in the corridor, not at Mrs Arora's as instructed. Waves of relief swept over her children as she emerged from the room. Reshmi had found Sid's mobile and dropped it into Jasmine's bag as they exited the penthouse.

They were free. Nothing could dilute that sense of freedom—not even the fact that Sid hadn't come for them.

CHAPTER TWELVE

The tiny hut, dwarfed by tall trees and willowy branches, was barely noticeable in that narrow street. A crowd of curious children lingered outside, whispering as they watched the tall, and handsome man who had come in a chauffeured car to visit *Pāṭṭi* Saroja. Their parents had told them that it was Pāṭṭi's son, but they couldn't believe it. The man seemed rich and educated. Why would he have left poor Pāṭṭi alone?

They eyed the white Mercedes Benz with awe. The driver stood outside, guarding it like the missionaries guarded the altar. Why was he not letting them run their hands down the bonnet? It wasn't as if they were going to scratch it. Maybe if they offered the driver a cup of tea, he would take them for a ride?

What hope! He turned as they were running their hands on the roof and growled in Tamil, *"Kārai toṭātē."* They scrambled from there, shrieking with fright.

Sid shed his coat as the interior of the hut was warm. But none of the discomfort registered. All he could think of was that he had found his mother. Sid burrowed in his mother's lap, inhaling the soft fragrance of her sari and the odour of spices that clung to it. He wished he had found his mother earlier. Maybe he should have put far more effort into tracing her; he shouldn't have left it so long. How had she survived in such living conditions?

But he was thankful God had kept his mother alive to see him. Her failing eyesight hadn't stopped her from admiring Sid, listening to all he had achieved and crying with happiness. She informed all the neighbours that her long-lost son was coming to see her, and inquisitive heads peeped inside, watching the huge man lying on the floor with his head on his mother's lap.

The white Mercedes was already attracting attention; the driver was shooing the children away as they came to inspect the vehicle. Maybe Sid should ask him to take those kids for a drive. He remembered the day the Chevaliers had come to get him. They, too, had come in a beautiful vehicle. At first, Sid hadn't stopped admiring the long, sleek form and studying the cream and gold interiors. The Chevaliers had smiled and said they had more beautiful luxuries for him in France. The smile had faded from Sid's face, and he had darted into the hut and hugged his mother. Only then did he realise why his mother had always been crying and his father had been extra nice to him.

The hut was similar to the one Sid had lived in, and he looked around him, trying to remember the furniture. The rope bed in a diamond design was still there; his mother had weaved that for Sid. How excited he had been to have a bed for himself. He blinked in horror as his eyes turned watery. Not now. He had finally reunited with his mother. This was no time for tears.

His mother had been waiting at the door, bent over her stick, her thinning grey hair oiled and braided. Her face was lined with years of hardship and suffering, but the smile was full even if there weren't many teeth left. Sid had lifted his mother off the ground and circled the place, his happiness so contagious that everyone had stopped working to watch mother and son laugh and cry together.

He had learned how Becka had been in touch with his mother and had promised to arrange a meeting with Sid if the details his mother gave were right. Since Becka hadn't returned, Sid's mother became impatient and called the office as Becka had left her visiting card.

"I missed you so much, Amma. The Chevaliers wouldn't tell me where you were."

"How could they, Siddhu? They were your legal parents. They paid a large sum of money to your father. It was the only way to save you."

"After a while, I stopped asking about you. I tried to be the son they wanted, but I couldn't forget you, Amma. They couldn't take your place."

"Forgive me, Siddhu, I don't regret giving you up. Your father would have killed you had you stayed here. What would you have become? A coolie? A drunkard and woman beater like your father? Look at you now, how far you've come. The Chevaliers educated you."

"I don't know, Amma. I'd have at least had you with me." His voice wobbled, feeling helpless as tears streaked his face. "But you're right; I never lacked in any way. However, every time I achieved something, I thought of you, and the past would return to haunt me."

Her soft hands wiped his face, and he cried more, thinking of the times she used to dab at his eyes with her sari pallu.

"There wasn't a day I didn't cry, Siddhu. I wondered about you and how you were doing. From time to time, Father Pius would tell me how well you were doing. He said I should leave you alone."

"Is he alive, Amma? I wrote to him asking about you, but I got no response."

"He is no more, Siddhu. After his passing, no one gave any news about you. But they were kind to me. When your father lavishly spent everything we had and left me in debt, the missionaries gave me this hut, and occasionally, sent me provisions."

"Where did you call from, Amma? I didn't see any phone booths around."

"I went to town."

"But that's a half-an-hour trek on foot? You must have

been exhausted?"

"Not after hearing your voice, Siddhu," she said, shifting his head from her lap to the pillow beside her. Sid brought his head back on her lap, and she smiled as she combed her fingers through his hair, filling him up on everything that had happened post-separation. Lavanya, the girl next door, took care of his mother. Her voice turned soft with regret as she told Sid that Lavanya would have made him a lovely wife, but she got married last year.

Sid heaved a sigh of relief. There was no saying what his mother would have done had Lavanya been unmarried. Thank goodness he'd escaped that trap. He remembered how Lavanya and he had played together. One of their favourite games was chasing a bicycle tyre with sticks in their hands. Lavanya had a particular fondness for the garden wheelbarrow. They would steal into the nearest school campus, where a rusty wheelbarrow leaned against the wall. Lavanya would get into it, and Sid would push it around the campus. One day, the gardener chased them, and they escaped by the skin of their teeth.

His mind strayed to Jasmine. Would Roy have followed up on the case? Not that he doubted his dependability, but he was feeling uneasy over leaving in such a hurry without personally ensuring that Jasmine and her children were safe. At least if his mobile was with him, he could have laid his mind at rest. He felt awful that he hadn't kept his promise to Jasmine and the girls. But when he explained it all to Jasmine, she would understand.

"Did the Chevaliers treat you well, Siddhu?"

Sid looked at his mother, trying to assimilate his thoughts. He would think of Jasmine later when he got back to Delhi. He couldn't do much from here anyway, not without a phone.

"I wasn't a good son to them, Amma. They tried very hard to undo the past, but it was impossible. All I saw was you. I hated them touching me, bathing me, feeding me."

"I didn't want to give you away, Siddhu. That night when you cried, begging me to let you stay, I was tempted to change my mind. But look at you now! Would you have become what you are today if I hadn't given you away? Your appa would have put you on the street. We must thank God for turning you into such a great officer. We must thank the Chevaliers for educating you."

"Yes, Amma, I'm grateful to them. I'll call and talk to them. Now that I've found you, I'm free from the past. I can love again."

"And have you found a woman to love?" She looked at him expectantly, her nearly blinded eyes shining with pride.

Sid was glad she had introduced the topic as he had wondered how to bring up the subject of Jasmine and her children.

"Yes, Amma, a very beautiful woman. I rescued her from a brutal man like Appa. You will love her."

The smile slowly vanished from his mother's face. The gnarled fingers stopped caressing his hair. "Rebecca is married?"

"No, Becka is my assistant. I'm talking about my woman. Her name is Jasmine. I want to adopt her daughters and have a family, Amma."

She looked at Sid, horrified, one hand going to her mouth. "Siddhu, my boy, she belongs to another man. You cannot separate them because you want her. I didn't bring you into this world to destroy a family." Her forehead creased, and there was disappointment on her face. "Is she older than you?"

"It doesn't matter to me, Amma."

"Why, Siddhu? You can have the best of girls with your looks, money, and position. Why a senior married woman with children?"

"Jasmine is good for me, Amma."

"Even that Becka girl is better. She took such trouble to find me. She must love you very much to do this for you."

Sid's head shifted from his mother's lap, and he sat up. He couldn't bear the thought that Jasmine was being judged just because she was married with children and older than him. He had to make it clear to his mother that this was his life and he would choose whom to marry.

It pained him to see the worry on his mother's face, however, he wouldn't let anyone come in the way of Jasmine and him.

"Siddhu?"

"I failed her, Amma. I promised her security and left her and her children in that madman's grasp while I came in search of you." He closed his eyes and swore, thinking of the journey back. Roy had booked an open return ticket for Sid and a one-way ticket for his mother. But before that, he would have to convince his mother to go with him.

His mother was shaking her head even before he asked her. Cupping his face in her trembling hands, she said, "No, Siddhu, this is my home. I will die if you take me from here. This is all I have, *kanna*. You go back and find your Jasmine and help her and her children. Your life is in Delhi. Mine is here."

"I can't leave you, Amma. No way. You are all I have. I want to take care of you. I want you with me forever."

"You have a family already, Siddhu. Jasmine and her children will take up most of your time. You have rescue operations to run. Go back, Siddhu. I can manage on my own."

Sid shook his head. He was damned if he was leaving his mother behind to fend for herself. Bad enough, he felt guilty for leaving it so long, although he wasn't to blame. But seeing the deplorable conditions in which she lived, he was upset with his adoptive parents for being tight-lipped about his mother's whereabouts.

He took her frail body in his arms and hugged her. "I'm not leaving you again. Either you come with me, or I'll give up everything and come and stay with you in this hut. Do you want that?"

"And Jasmine?"

Sid gave a tight smile. He wasn't going to speak about Jasmine. Once the two women met, things would change. He was certain Jasmine would adore his mother and his mother would love Jasmine. As for Reshmi and Mira, they would find a way to his mother's heart. They spoke a common language as their extended family came from Pondicherry. His mother would be thrilled to talk Tamil in Delhi. He was sure of that. Coming to think of it, even he hadn't forgotten his Tamil!

"How many days do you need to pack your things and inform your friends?"

"Only Lavanya needs to know. Why don't you go and see her while I pack up? She'll be happy. She always said you'll be back."

Sid nodded. He, too, wanted to meet Lavanya. He was indebted to her for taking care of his mother. Had she hoped Sid would come back for her? She used to have a major crush on Sid and followed him everywhere. He would leave Lavanya a handsome cheque. Also, he had to repay the missionaries for providing food and shelter for his mother. He hadn't forgotten how Father Pius had taken him in whenever Sid's father had kicked him out. Sid decided to generously contribute to the missionary's good work.

CHAPTER THIRTEEN

Jasmine vaguely remembered the area where Sid resided and struggled to recall the landmarks. Mrs Arora had booked them into a guest house for the night as she felt it was dangerous for Jasmine and the children to be on their own. The kind woman then arranged for a chauffeured car to drop them off at the outskirts of Sid's villa. They didn't want the chauffeur to know where they were heading in case he was questioned.

Reshmi and Mira were excited to be on foot as they had never experienced walking in the streets. The three of them squatted on a bench at a tea stall en route and ordered tea and snacks.

A goat was feeding on dried leaves, and Mira went to inspect what she could do about his diet. Reshmi questioned the stall owner about his customers and whether the business was doing well. Jasmine sat in pensive silence, planning the future. She had to find a job quickly and enrol her children in school. Then, she should meet Advocate Chowdary and see if she could gain full custody of her children.

The tea stall owner served tea with a plate of steaming samosas freshly scooped from the tava. He left the ketchup sauce bottle on the small makeshift table when he saw Mira and Reshmi licking their fingers. There was no news from Sid or Rescue Operations, but that didn't deter Jasmine from enjoying her freedom. She understood Sid could not get in touch as his mobile was with them and Reshmi's mobile was with Rebecca. Jasmine never had a mobile as Sunil hadn't provided her with one. He worried that Jasmine would tell people about what was going on.

"Do you think I should call Sid's office?" Reshmi asked as she took a bite of her samosa, dipped liberally in ketchup. "I find it odd he didn't come for us, Mom. It's not like him."

"Maybe he doesn't know?" Jasmine replied as she fed Mira from her plate and the goat who came inspecting. He nosed through Jasmine's bag, found a stale tomato lettuce sandwich, and gobbled it up. Then he searched for a water basin, and without permission, dipped his head and quenched his thirst.

"Can we take him with us?" Mira asked. "He will have a lot of food in Uncle Sid's garden."

Jasmine didn't think Sid would appreciate a greedy black goat nipping at his well-mowed lawn. "His mother will miss him. I'll tell you what, we'll ask the tea man to take care of him and leave some money for his welfare."

Jasmine paid for the tea and samosas. Of course, she didn't believe that Sid didn't know. The villa security guards would have informed him of the break-in and kidnap.

"Maybe he is with Rebecca in the hospital," Jasmine said. Her heart constricted, her imagination running riot with memories of Sid's tender loving. What if he was tending to his beautiful assistant at this very moment?

"Yes, Mom. Pop's men bruised her badly. I saw the whole thing," Reshmi said.

"Sid claimed she's a black belt?"

"Yes... and deserves the title. She fought several heavily armed guards single-handed, Mom. Here and there, I chipped in, but there were too many. Why don't we call Roy? Apparently, he's pretty close to Rebecca. She said he had a major crush on her."

Jasmine wasn't sure it was a good idea. There was something about the retired police officer that made her nervous. He hadn't been very encouraging when Jasmine had called the office before she and Mira were kidnapped. She had wanted to talk to Sid and tell him that whatever might happen in the future, she would never forget what he had done for them. Don't ask her why she needed to do that. Maybe somewhere in the back of her mind, she had a premonition that their happiness was about to end. But Roy had been brusque. The boss wasn't in the office, and whatever Jasmine wanted to tell him could wait until Sid returned to the villa.

She watched Reshmi as she punched the Rescue Operations number using Sid's mobile. She guessed it was Roy who picked up the phone. She figured he was saying something harsh to Reshmi. Her dark eyes were moist by the end of the conversation.

Jasmine took the phone from Reshmi's numb hands, her only thought being she would not let anyone bully them again. Sending Reshmi for a walk with Mira, she said, "I would like to talk with Mr Chevalier. This is Mrs Chari."

"He is not in the office."

"Is there any way I could reach him?"

"Why? Haven't you done enough?" he asked in frigid tones. "We almost lost a bright young officer because of you. Sid's villa is completely damaged. Our office is receiving threatening emails and phone calls from your husband's cronies. What more do you want?"

Jasmine wiped her eyes discreetly. "I'm sorry. I will ensure Sunil pays for the damages for Mr Chevalier's villa and also Rebecca's hospital bills. I never thought my husband would stoop so low."

"Okay, done," Roy said.

"Did Mr Chevalier know we'd been kidnapped?"

"Yes, Mrs Chari. I was there when he received the call from Mashraf." His voice seemed cool, calm, and unfriendly.

Jasmine rubbed her temples. "Is he okay?"

"Quite fine, Mrs Chari, but very busy. We have other cases, you know."

Jasmine shivered as she felt a chill seep into her bones. She wasn't going to panic. She was a survivor. Nothing could break her. She would not allow it.

"Sorry to have bothered you. We won't trouble Rescue Operations anymore."

"Good luck, Mrs Chari. Advocate Chowdary will be in touch with you."

"Thank you."

"Can you drop Sid's mobile at the office?"

"We'll deliver it to the villa security at the gate," Jasmine said.

"That won't be necessary. I'll have someone pick it up."

"No, we are not too far from the villa. We'll drop it with the security. I'm glad we spoke to you before landing there. You see, we had no idea we were bothering Mr Chevalier."

"Let me know if I can be of help."

She knew he was merely being polite. The last thing Roy wanted was to help them. It was so obvious in his tone. She couldn't blame him.

Jasmine thanked the tea stall owner and continued to walk in the direction Reshmi and Mira had taken. Her daughters spied her from a distance and rushed towards her, sensing her weary state. *We are with you*, they seemed to say, *and wherever you take us, we will go.*

Jasmine didn't realise she was crying. She felt as if their world had collapsed. While earlier they had marched with enthusiasm towards Sid's residence, now their steps lagged. Not even the chirping birds and swaying branches could lighten their heavy hearts.

They heard the growl of the Porsche and swiftly cut through the expansive lawn, seeking shelter under a cluster of trees. Jasmine held onto her children and ducked behind the thick shrubs, her heart racing as she spotted the approaching silver-grey monster purring to a halt near the villa.

She wept with relief as Sid slid out. He was safe. She longed to run into his arms and take refuge, but she couldn't indulge in that luxury anymore. She watched him open the passenger door and help Rebecca from the car. His arm slid around her as she adjusted the crutches, and they walked towards the entrance. *It is over.* Jasmine's one night with Sid was just that—one night of tenderness. She would cherish it forever.

Jasmine realised she was clutching Reshmi and Mira, and they gave her a quick upward glance. There was comprehension there. Reshmi's hands clenched at her side, while Mira whispered, "Uncle Sid... Uncle Sid."

Jasmine felt such heaviness in her chest that even her breathing became difficult. Sid returned to the car and helped an elderly woman with a bundle in her arms. The woman was looking around her in awe. What puzzled Jasmine was how Sid held her to his side and talked to her as he led her inside the villa.

There was a striking resemblance between them, and Jasmine frowned in confusion. Was she a relative? Was she in some kind of trouble? Was that what had held him—the reason why he couldn't come to rescue Jasmine and her children? But wouldn't Roy have told her if that were so?

It was time to leave. Reshmi went to deposit Sid's mobile. Mira tagged along. Jasmine stayed where she was, her eyes on the portico to glimpse Sid. He came out a few minutes later, jumped into his car, and sped past her. Jasmine felt such a longing in her heart that if it wasn't for Rebecca and the elderly lady, she would have forgotten herself and gone running behind Sid shamelessly.

Why had he not kept his promise? What could have made him forget them?

She could see the portico from this side of the garden. Rebecca limped out using her crutches and sat on the swing chair, rocking herself slowly with a wide smile. It appeared she was finally getting the attention she had wanted. Jasmine couldn't help the jealousy that overwhelmed her at the thought of Rebecca in Sid's bed.

Reshmi and Mira had returned and watched Rebecca for a while. Even Mira kept silent.

"Let's go, Mom; there's no place for us here," Reshmi said.

Jasmine examined her face, knowing how fond of Sid her daughters were, and for Reshmi to take such a decision meant she had given up on him.

Mira looked at her mother and said innocently, "Akka and I climbed on the rail. Uncle Sid and Becka Aunty were kissing."

"Shut up!" Reshmi snarled. "He was not kissing her. She kissed him, and he was too polite to push her away."

Jasmine's heart thudded as she lifted Mira onto her hip and placed her arm around Reshmi. They walked back, taking the same route; only, it seemed longer and more tiring.

The goat was sitting quietly by the tea shop, but when he saw them, he got up and accompanied them until the end of the road.

Reshmi dialled Mrs Arora, and they chatted for a while. Mrs Arora promised to find them accommodation. She was their only hope now. And once they had a roof over their head, Jasmine would find a job and send Reshmi to school. Mira could skip nursery. It was too expensive.

CHAPTER FOURTEEN

Sid slumped on the executive chair of his cabin and attacked his mail. His table was piled with files. He glanced briefly at them, but his mind kept shifting from one situation to another. None of his contacts knew anything about Mrs Chari and her children. He must call Sunil, as much as he was reluctant to do so, and find out about Jasmine.

Five minutes later, he gave a loud, frustrated sigh. He couldn't believe what Sunil had told him. How could the petrified Jasmine stand up for herself and threaten him? Sid found himself smiling despite his tension. No wonder Sunil was so angry. He swore to do everything he could to ruin his wife and fight for custody of Mira.

Something, however, nagged Sid. Why had Jasmine not returned to the villa? Even if she didn't know the address, she had the office numbers, and it was close to Residency Towers. Surely, she could have googled and found the information? Why had Reshmi not contacted the bureau? She would never have let her mother's decisions stop her from getting in touch.

Roy seemed tight-lipped whenever the subject of Jasmine came up. Sid couldn't place his finger on it yet, but he would get to the bottom of it. Knowing Roy, he was probably peeved that Jasmine and her daughters had escaped before he organised the rescue.

Sid rubbed at his temples, feeling the strain of the last few hours as he stretched tiredly on his chair. He had to call Advocate Chowdary and set up a meeting.

The landline rang. He grabbed the receiver, but it was not

Jasmine. His mobile had been delivered to the gated security officer, he was told. Sid sat up. Jasmine and her daughters had come to the villa. Hell! Did they see him with Becka... his arm around her, taking her inside? Could Reshmi have seen Becka making another play for him?

Sid groaned aloud. Damn! He should have followed his instincts when he'd felt such a strong, prickling sensation at the back of his neck. He'd thought he had imagined it. Had three pairs of eyes observed Sid all that time he'd walked Becka and his mother to his residence? What must they be thinking, particularly as he hadn't come to their rescue as promised?

He turned to Roy once again, noticing how he was avoiding looking at him. It was not like Roy not to ask about his mother. What was he hiding? Did he know something?

"Did Jess call?"

Roy's broad shoulders sagged, and he nodded, continuing his work. Sid breathed slowly, trying to control himself. *Jess had called, and Roy didn't tell him. Why?*

"She asked where you were. I told her."

Sid shot out of his chair, an insurmountable rage enveloping him. Why had he hidden this information from him? He knew he was looking for Jasmine. Damn it! Everyone knew. Sid had turned the office upside down trying to locate her.

"What exactly did you tell her, Roy?"

Roy gave a long, heavy sigh as he came around the desk and sat on the edge, his legs folded at the ankles. "I asked if she needed any help, and she said she could manage."

"You asked if she needed..." His voice furiously repeated what Roy said, only in soft, dangerous tones. "You knew she needed help! I told you to arrange their rescue, and despite that, you didn't rescue them and then asked if she needed...?"

"She sounded okay, boss."

"Did she? And how would you know? Did you see her?

How about her children? Did you enquire if they had a roof? Food on the table?" Sid felt his hands clench with such fury that he had to move away before he did something he'd regret.

Anna was staring at them with her mouth open. She had wanted to tell her boss about the calls, but Roy said he would take care of it. Apparently, he hadn't, and now the boss would be mad at her.

"Well, Roy, you are fired. Right now. Take yourself out of my sight. I don't want to see you again."

Roy turned pale. He rose from his lounging position, realising that his boss was dead serious. "You don't mean that, boss. I've been with you since the inception of this bureau."

"You are not a part of it anymore. Leave."

Sid stood with his back turned towards him, not wanting to see his face or even say goodbye. He had depended on Roy, who had worked without prejudice in the past, so why should he have erred in this case? How could he have ignored Sid's instructions? Supposing Sunil had done something horribly insane. There were enough cases where the irate husband threw acid on his wife's face.

Roy staggered to his desk and dropped onto the chair, his expression grey. Without another word, he started to pack his things. Bitterness welled up within. Sid was firing him for considering his safety? What injustice was this? Roy emptied the items on his table into a cardboard box Anna hurriedly brought him. She seemed as shocked as him and scampered to her desk, worried she might be next on the list.

Sid paced his office, trying to think of a way to undo the damage. God knew what Roy would have told Jasmine. No wonder she hadn't contacted him. And when she had come to the villa, she'd have seen Becka and decided not to trouble him anymore. No wonder Roy had insisted that Sid pick Becka up from the hospital on his way from the airport. He must have known Jasmine would be heading to the villa to drop off the mobile and had counted on her seeing him with Becka.

Things were beginning to fall into place. Roy had made no attempt to rescue Jasmine. He had sent Sid to Pondicherry happily, knowing the presence of Sid's mother would make him forget everything else.

"I thought I was protecting you, boss," Roy said as he carried the carton to the exit. "She's married with children and senior by six years. She has a powerful husband who could ruin you and your business. What's more, he could claim you molested his minor daughters. And you are sacking me because I had your interests at heart?"

"If I don't find Jess and her children, you can be sure you won't live to find another job!" Sid rose and strode to the door. He had to question security. Find out if they had any details of Jasmine. From what they had described, Reshmi and Mira had approached them. Jasmine must have been watching from afar. He knew what she'd be thinking—that she was not right for Sid, and seeing him with Becka and his mother would have just reconfirmed her decision.

Sid was still seething when he returned to the villa that evening and slammed the door behind him, startling Rebecca and his mother from their deep exchange. He walked straight to his bedroom without greeting either of them. That Sid looked haggard was another matter. Rebecca looked at Sid's mother and made a face. She smiled back, patting her hand.

Rebecca knew the reason for Sid's mood because Roy had briefed her earlier. She was as stunned as Roy had been that Sid had sent him packing. Rebecca knew she would be next if Sid guessed that she and Roy had planned her arrival at the villa. Roy had told her about Mrs Chari's call and how she insisted on dropping off Sid's phone with the villa's security. He was frantic about Sid falling into Mrs Chari's web once again. Rebecca then considered playing on Sid's emotions and asked if she could recuperate at his place. After all, Sid's mother was now with him, and she would feel lonely in a strange place. Rebecca offered to keep her company. Put that way, Sid could hardly refuse.

What Rebecca hadn't counted on was that Saroja would take to her. Despite the cultural barrier, she seemed to like Rebecca and was rooting for her to marry Sid. But Sid's proposal was a distant dream. If Rebecca wanted something to happen between them, it should be before he found Mrs Chari again.

Rebecca looked at Mrs Saroja with a rueful smile. The elderly lady made signs to her to go after him. Rebecca excused herself, and under the watchful gaze of the old lady, drew herself up with difficulty, dragged the crutches under her arms, and hobbled towards the bedroom. She was tired of Sid treating her like dirt. It was about time he acknowledged her love. With a set expression, she knocked, and hearing no response, opened the door.

Sid controlled his exasperation as he heard movement in his bedroom. He wasn't stupid. It was Becka. His mother would never walk into his room. He was sorry for treating his mother brusquely, but he was upset with her for encouraging Becka to hope when she knew that he loved Jasmine.

Sid didn't wait to dry off before pulling on his robe and striding out of the washroom. His expression turned thunderous when he saw Becka's shapely body lying naked on his bed. Why was she so thick-skinned? Hadn't he threatened to sack her if she tried that stunt again? Did she imagine there was more to it because he had agreed to her proposition to recuperate at the villa?

"Get out, Becka. I need my sleep." He looked at her impatiently, cursing himself for letting her stay at the villa. His guilt that Sunil's men had bruised Becka was the only reason he had agreed. He had wanted to make it up to Becka and help her get back on her feet. But apparently, his actions were misunderstood.

He dragged the bed cover back and got under, his mind wandering to Jasmine and the night they spent. He wondered how she was managing alone with her daughters with possibly not much money on her.

Why couldn't she call him? He had collected his phone from the security personnel and some further details about them, but not enough to track them down. All he could do was hope that Jasmine had contacted the advocate. He had left the card with her.

Becka continued to lie beside him, her luscious body enticingly available for Sid if he wanted. Sid sat up irritably, looking at the beautiful picture she made on his bed. "I meant it, Becka. Go, before I throw you out. I can't deal with this now."

Rebecca sat up slowly, her high cheekbones pink with embarrassment. She tied her robe that she had confidently untied earlier, thinking she could seduce him.

"Why do you want *her*? What's wrong with me? I can give you much more than Mrs Chari. Even your mother thinks the same."

"My mother doesn't decide for me, Becka. I'm sorry. I was clear with you right from the start. I'm not interested in you in that way."

"If Mrs Chari had not come in the way, you'd have eventually given in."

"No! I don't think so, Becka. I've never loved you in that way and never will. Don't waste your time on me." Sid's tone turned gentle as she bent her head, her pale hair falling softly on her slender shoulders. "Roy has been in love with you for years. Give him a chance."

Rebecca felt humiliated as she lifted her aching body from the bed and gathered her crutches.

Sid turned away and stared at the wall, feeling guilty for hurting her. Could he have been giving her contradictory signals all these years? He didn't think so.

When Sid had begun Rescue Operations, Becka had come to know and had applied for the post of 'Trained Investigative

Officer'. She had reminded Sid of their encounter in France and how they had fought on the eve of the tournament. Of course, Sid remembered Becka. Who wouldn't? But he explained he couldn't consider her application as he doubted he could work with someone who seemed to fancy herself in love with him. Becka had laughed heartily and told him he had a fat ego. And then she explained why she needed the job. She told Sid about her stepfather and how he had ruined her childhood. She aimed to put men like her stepfather and other horrible men behind bars. Sid hadn't hesitated to recruit Becka after that.

Thinking of Roy made Sid feel worse. He had treated him badly, and there was no excuse, however angry he had been. Sid would have to rectify that tomorrow, along with a bouquet for Becka. He couldn't afford to lose them professionally.

CHAPTER FIFTEEN

As Sid walked into the bureau the next morning, Advocate Chowdary awaited him. Anna was at her desk, busily handling callers and liaising with the other rescue officers. Roy and Becka's absence felt strange, and Sid was already working on his apology.

Roy must have contacted Advocate Chowdary to rectify his uncooperative behaviour. Sid breathed deeply. He was one step closer to locating Jasmine. He hadn't slept a wink the previous night as his thoughts had been on Jasmine and her daughters. Not even his mother's presence could soften his mood.

"I want that bastard behind bars," Sid informed the advocate as he took his place at his desk, leaning forward with his elbows resting on the bureau. He'd have to get the ball running before Sunil moved. He didn't believe that hogwash about not pressing charges on Jasmine and only wanting custody of Mira. Sid had been too long in this business to know when a man was lying. And Sunil was.

Advocate Chowdary had represented several cases concerning abused women, particularly those sent by Sid. There was nothing new about this case except that the French officer seemed rather stressed about it. Advocate Chowdary shuddered. The young chief looked like he had murder in mind.

"She must want it too, Officer," he told Sid in firm tones. "From what I gather, she's fighting only for custody of her children—nothing else."

Sid's head jerked, and the chair swirled as he grabbed Advocate Chowdary's arm. "You spoke to Jasmine? *When*?"

Advocate Chowdary frowned at Sid and pried open the grip around his arm, revising his opinion of the French officer. He was *terribly* stressed. Chowdary wasn't sure he was safe in his presence.

"This morning!"

"But how did you? I mean..." Sid breathed deeply, wishing Mr Chowdary would just tell him all about it instead of waiting for him to ask questions. "I couldn't get Mrs Chari on the phone. You know how it is in this job. I've been trying since yesterday."

"Well, I told her to come to my office tomorrow. We need to discuss the case in detail. She has signed off her rights, and that is complicating the case."

"What time is your meeting?" Sid asked, trying to keep his voice casual.

Advocate Chowdary was packing his briefcase, seemingly in a hurry to leave. But something about Sid's expression made him pause.

"Mrs Chari told me how you helped her, and she and her children owe their lives to you."

Sid didn't reply. He didn't think he deserved praise. He should have been with them when Sunil had arrived. This was the punishment he merited for not having kept his promise.

"The meeting is at 10:00 a.m."

He didn't think Jasmine would want to speak to him tomorrow, but he was going to make sure he was there by her side—if not for Jasmine, then at least for her children.

Sid continued to take calls, offshoring the tasks to an outside agency while keeping track of everything that was happening. He couldn't go personally to rescue the women as there was quite a lot of Roy and Becka's pending work. And then he had Jasmine's case on his mind, and he wouldn't rest until he got her and her children out of Sunil's radar.

*

Saroja was sitting in the backyard, staring at the horizon, feeling a deep sense of loneliness. After Rebecca left, her son's mood had lightened; however, he seemed to be tense about that married woman and her children. Without knowing the woman, Saroja began to dislike her intensely. Why should she tie her son in knots when she had a life of her own? Saroja was starting to miss Pondicherry and her life in that little hut. She hadn't had much there, but those people spoke her language and made her feel at home. Here, she was lost and alone. Not that Siddhu denied her anything…

Saroja had a chauffeured car whenever she wanted to go to the market, but unfortunately, there was no one to accompany her. The driver spoke only Hindi and took Saroja to expensive locations that made her feel out of place. This morning, she asked him to take her to the underground market Rebecca had told her about – Palika Bazaar. Amit said it was dangerous to be alone and accompanied her there. Saroja had enjoyed the trip, and she and Amit drank sherbet and had lunch in one of the hole-in-the-wall eat-out places. More than three hundred shops easily sold various items, mostly electronics and clothing. She bought some cotton nightdresses for herself, some harem pants for Rebecca, and a white body shirt for Siddhu. The shopkeeper said it was cotton stretch and would suit a muscled man.

Saroja was startled out of her reverie when she heard a child giggling. A little girl suddenly appeared out of nowhere, kicking a ball in Saroja's direction and running behind it. Saroja wondered from which villa the girl had emerged as there weren't many in the vicinity, except the villa of Mrs Singh, an elderly lady who stayed alone. Mrs Singh's son was in the USA. Her lawn and Siddhu's were adjoined, but Siddhu had planted trees around the property, guarding his privacy.

Could it be Mrs Singh's granddaughter? How did the little girl manage to come into their garden? Not that Saroja was about to complain. Any company was better than no company! The girl seemed in a world of her own and didn't notice Saroja until she was almost on top of her. She stopped suddenly and gave Saroja such a sweet smile that Saroja's heart melted.

"My name is Mira. What is yours?" she asked Saroja in Tamil.

Saroja almost fell off her chair in delight. She drew the girl towards her and questioned her about her parents and where she had come from. She rattled off in Tamil, and Saroja wanted to hug her.

"Amma speaks Tamil," she said.

"Does she?" Saroja's interest perked, looking around them for the absent woman. "Is your amma living close by?"

Mira shook her head, losing some of her enthusiasm. She kicked the ball hard and sent it across the garden. "Amma is caring for Pāṭṭi." She pointed to Mrs Singh's house.

So, Saroja was right. It was Mrs Singh's granddaughter.

"I play outside where Amma can see me. Akka will come in the evening from school."

"What about your appa?"

"I don't have an appa."

Saroja frowned in confusion. Did Mrs Singh's son divorce his wife? Surely, Siddhu would have known?

"Do you want to play with me?" she asked Saroja.

There was a hopeful tilt of her head as she contemplated Saroja. Saroja smiled, her mind still preoccupied with whose daughter this child could be.

"Are you Mrs Singh's granddaughter?"

"No. Amma works for Pāṭṭi."

Saroja felt ashamed of her discontent. This poor child was barely five and had accepted her fate, and Saroja was cribbing about not having someone to talk with. Shouldn't she be happy to have found her son and live with him in this beautiful villa?

Saroja's loneliness vanished, and she watched with a smile as Mira ran after the ball. She hoped she would meet Mira's family as she was anxious to talk with them in her native tongue, amongst other things. Perhaps they could employ Mira's mother so she could earn a little more for her family. She'd run the idea by Siddhu; she was certain he would agree. Her son was very generous; Lavanya told Saroja in her last call about the cheque Siddhu had given her. Then, the missionaries wrote to Saroja, telling her how her son had paid for the church's renovation.

Her attention shifted to Mira, and she had to say she was a well-behaved child and spoke fine Tamil, not the local Tamil. Could she be from a privileged background and had fallen on hard times? That would explain how her mother became a caretaker. Maybe she could ask Siddhu to enquire, and if possible, employ that poor woman in his office. That way, he could lessen the load. From the time his colleagues had left, Siddhu came home tired and depressed.

Mira was coming towards Saroja again, and another girl ran after her. She was pretty, too, with thick, black braids and white ribbons, just like the students in Pondicherry. Saroja stared at the children and felt nostalgic; they seemed so content chasing a colourful ball, and she wanted to keep them longer at her side. How did they manage to be so joyful despite not having a father and their mother working the whole day and possibly the night?

How she wished Siddhu could meet a nice woman and give Saroja grandchildren.

"This is my akka Reshmi. She is in standard six. I'm too little to go to school, Amma said."

Saroja took the children inside, and they looked around them with delight. Saroja made them comfortable and went in search of some eatables. They seemed hungry and wolfed down the biscuits on the plate. She wondered if Siddhu would mind that she had invited the children to his villa in his absence. But she forgot all about it as the children chatted with her in Tamil. She learnt more about their situation, but they were not very talkative. What beautiful, well-behaved children!

Suddenly, a woman called out to them, and they were startled. Gulping the tea, they rose, kissed Saroja's cheeks, and rushed out without leaving their contact number. Saroja hoped they would return the next day, or she would trouble Mrs Singh with a visit.

When Sid came home that evening, he observed that his mother seemed in good humour as he threw his coat over the back of the chair. She was smiling for the first time since her arrival, and he wondered what could have put her in such a good mood. He was smiling, too, as he would see Jasmine the next day. He missed her and her adorable daughters.

"How was your day?" Sid asked his mother, dragging the shirt off his body as he sauntered to the bedroom. Normally, it would start with complaints about her loneliness and whether she should go to Pondicherry for a few days. But not this evening.

His mother followed him to the washroom and watched with curiosity as he stripped his trousers off and stepped into the shower in his underwear. She spoke through the sound of running water.

"I bought you a white T-shirt at Palika Bazaar."

"Ah! That's why you're so happy. You felt at home there," he teased, turning off the shower as he began soaping himself.

"I enjoyed the outing, Siddhu. Amit and I had parathas, chaat, butter chicken, kebabs, *chole bhature*, biryani, rolls, samosa, and *gol gappa*..."

"Amma, you ate all that? What an appetite you have!"

"Small portions of each, Siddhu. I wanted to taste Delhi food."

Sid was scrubbing his back and arms when his ears perked

up at something she said.

"—Two young visitors, Reshmi and Mira."

The soap slipped through his fingers, and he rushed out of the cubicle and pulled his mother inside. She gave a yelp when he turned on the shower and hot spray rained on her.

"You're wetting me."

"Did you like them?" he asked, washing the soap off his body, his excitement mounting as she laughed and ran out of the steamy cabin, squeezing the excess water from her sari. Sid, in the meantime, couldn't stop smiling. He would get it out of Reshmi tomorrow; he was certain it was her brilliant idea.

Did that mean they were missing him? That they had forgiven him? That they wanted him in their circle?

Saroja broke into a sweet smile. "They spoke in Tamil, Siddhu. What adorable children. I hope they come back tomorrow. I brought them inside and gave them something to eat. You don't mind, do you?"

"Didn't their mother come too?" *Thank you, Reshmi*, Sid muttered under his breath, knowing that it was her idea they speak in Tamil to his mother. Sid had already penned her as super-intelligent right from day one.

"A woman called out to them, and they rushed out. It must have been their mother. Would she mind if I kept the little girl with me in the mornings? Mira told me she plays outside the whole day while her mother works at Mrs Singh's and Reshmi is at school."

Sid's heart ached for Jasmine. Without support from that bastard of a husband, without Rescue Operations behind her, she hadn't baulked at taking a lowly position. Her well-to-do family could have provided for her had they been informed, but he was certain Jasmine wanted to do this alone. Why, even Sid would have provided for her, but proud as she was, she preferred to work, earn, and feed her family.

How did she get that job? He was sure she wouldn't have

wanted to be anywhere in the vicinity of his villa. To think he had been looking for Jasmine all over the place, and she had been a stone's throw away from his premises! Could Reshmi have set that up, too?

He wasn't going to sleep tonight. If things went well, he'd bring them home to meet his mother tomorrow. Hopefully, his mother would realise that Jasmine was as wonderful as her children.

CHAPTER SIXTEEN

"Why can't we come with you, Mom?" Reshmi asked, upset that she was being excluded from the meeting with Advocate Chowdary. She'd appointed herself her mother's guardian and had expected to accompany her, but ever since they had begun staying on their own, her mother had stopped depending on Reshmi and had become self-reliant.

The first thing her mother did after she got an advance was to enrol Reshmi back in school. Mira played on her own while her mother was at work. The only fear her mother had was the fact that they weren't far from Sid's residence, and she'd warned Reshmi and Mira not to go anywhere close to his house. And the previous evening, when she'd found them in the vicinity of Sid's villa, she'd looked at them suspiciously, but they swore that they had been playing and the ball had bounced along the fence and they'd gone to pick it up.

If only their mother discovered what they'd been up to, there would be no saying how she would react. Reshmi and Mira decided they missed Sid too much to keep away from him, and when they found that Rebecca had left the premises, they seized the opportunity to meet Sid's mother.

Reshmi gave Mira some classes in Tamil and instructed her on how to converse with the old lady. She felt that the battle would be won faster if they could get Sid's mother on their side. How happy she'd been with them. Reshmi sighed. If only they could have met Sid, too. She could have found out first-hand the reason why he'd left them to fend on their own. But maybe a few more meetings with his mother, and she would spill the beans.

Reshmi was certain it had something to do with finding his mother. He'd never spoken of having a mother, and Mrs Saroja didn't seem too familiar with the house, which meant that she'd never visited her son. How odd! Could he have been separated from his mother?

Jasmine halted in front of the mirror of their one-bedroom apartment that Mrs Singh had offered along with the job. The salary wasn't much, but she had some money and managed to pay for the essentials. Mrs Arora had bought Reshmi's uniform, books, and shoes. However, Jasmine refused to allow her to pay the fees. She would reimburse Mrs Arora somehow.

"You have to go to school, Reshmi. You missed enough classes protecting me from your father. From now on, I'm taking control of my life. You and Mira deserve a nice, peaceful existence. I'm going to meet the advocate and make sure Sunil treats us well."

"That man didn't treat us well when we were with him. Where is he going to bother about us now that we have left him?" Reshmi said.

How right Reshmi was. Sunil would rather see them on the streets than loan them any money—even if it was Jasmine's money he was handling. How foolish she was. Maybe they should go to the bank and ask for a loan. But which bank would trust a single mother with two girls who didn't have a roof of her own?

"I'll find a way, Reshmi. Don't worry. You study well. You must have a good future. Don't be foolish like me and marry the first man your parents arrange for you. How I wish I had some experience in the job force before I got married; I wouldn't have had to take up a housekeeper's post."

"Mom, you can go to evening college. You can study and become what you always wanted to be. What's stopping you now?"

"Age! I'm an old horse now. No one wants to employ a thirty-six-year-old mother of two girls." She ruffled her daughter's hair and grinned. "Not that I'm complaining. It just seems so hard at times."

"I hope you're not thinking of going back?" Reshmi said after a while.

Jasmine shuddered. "Never! I stayed too long in that abusive relationship. I didn't leave because of that wretched bond, but now, even that doesn't frighten me anymore."

"And Sid, don't you miss him, Mom?"

Jasmine's heart beat faster. An image of Sid standing in front of her bare-chested, his chocolate eyes locked on hers, his lips curved into an inviting smile. She felt the back of her lids burn. It would have been wonderful if he had been waiting for them. But that was wishful thinking. Sid had been carried away by his emotions. She couldn't blame him for backing off. Who would be foolish enough to take on a married woman with children when the best of girls were available—definitely not a rich and handsome man of his standing? No, she had to forget Sid.

"Becka is not staying there anymore, Mom."

Jasmine's head jerked up, and her eyes found Reshmi's. Her instincts had screamed last evening that they had been up to something. How could they go behind her back and do what she had forbade them to?

"I told you to leave him alone. He has his life, and we have ours. If you spy on Sid again, I'll leave my job. We'll go far away from this locality."

"I didn't spy on him, Mom," Reshmi interrupted. "Mira's ball had rolled into their garden, and we went to fetch it. Becka's Audi wasn't in the car park."

Her mother was capable of carrying out her threat, Reshmi thought. As it was, convincing her mother to take up the job had been difficult. The moment her mother heard that the job was close to Sid's residence, she'd refused point blank. If only she knew the role Reshmi had played, she would disown her. But Reshmi couldn't find any other way of entering Sid's premises and making his mother's acquaintance, so she had done a little research and found out that there was an old lady in one of the residences—as luck would have it, in the next compound—who was looking for a caretaker.

Mrs Arora had given a reference for her mother, and Reshmi had bunked school and gone over to see Mrs Singh. She explained their situation briefly, cried a little, and said that since her mother took care of them very well, so she would definitely know how to take care of the elderly lady. Then she contacted Mrs Arora and asked her to tell her mother about the job as she didn't want her to become suspicious. Mrs Arora not only spoke to Jasmine and convinced her to take the job but she also talked to the employer and asked her not to mention the daughter's visit.

Now, all Reshmi had to do was get her mother to meet Sid's mother, and the rest would take care of itself. Sid's mother had welcomed Mira and Reshmi; she would like their mother, too.

"Go and get ready for school." Jasmine gave Reshmi a little push. "I'll be okay on my own, I promise."

"You look beautiful, Mom. I like your hair like that."

Jasmine nodded absent-mindedly as she got her documents in order. She was tense about the meeting for several reasons. She was doing something alone for the first time and worried she would mess up. It was years since she had plucked up the courage to stand up for what she wanted, and now, when the time had come, she was afraid.

Mr Chowdary's office was on MG Road, near the famous MG Mall. Jasmine trembled as she got down with the other commuters and hurried from the metro station. Her eyes were downcast as she didn't want to encounter any familiar faces. It was a stone's throw away from Residency Towers. But of course, the kind of people who lived there had chauffeured cars to commute, like Jasmine once did. Not that she missed the luxurious life. What she missed the most was having more money to spare for her children. Sometimes, she felt depressed that she was dragging her children into a rut. Reshmi and Mira, however, never cried or complained. They appeared to be doing everything in their power to keep Jasmine smiling.

Mr Chowdary rose as Mrs Chari walked into his office with her head held high. He was taken aback by her poise as most of the women he met were subdued. How had such a beautiful woman allowed herself to be treated in that way?

Jasmine was glad she decided to wear heels, which made her feel confident. She'd secured her hair in a low knot and wore a pretty pastel salwar kameez. The advocate was looking at her intently as if he was inspecting her soul. Jasmine stared back, deciding she was done with cowering. She was a grown, mature woman, and she would behave like one.

"May I sit down?" She took the chair directly opposite him and placed her file on the desk. He glanced through the documents, nodding in approval, particularly at the detailed story she had written from the time she had met her husband.

When Jasmine began writing her life story, she realised how very unfairly Sunil had treated her and how she had been partially responsible for being treated that way. By the time she had finished, Jasmine felt lighter and more capable of handling the future.

The door opened as they were discussing alimony, and Jasmine swirled as a gush of cold wind entered the room. The tall, handsome man looked very familiar, even if he had lost heaps of weight. His chocolate fudge eyes were eating her up in a way that made her cheeks turn pink.

"Hello, Jess!"

That husky voice, the smile he shot Jasmine, and the way he strode towards her as if he owned her, leaning down to brush his lips against her cheek, made her want to run from there. Her heart hammered when she felt those tender lips grazing the curve of her cheek... and all of that in front of an astonished advocate. Poor Mr Chowdary was looking pretty embarrassed.

The only thought in Jasmine's mind was how Sid had known she was coming here. Had Reshmi told him? She'd disown her if she had, Jasmine thought in irritation. Why couldn't they get it into their heads that Sid had his own life to live?

No wonder Reshmi had looked so disappointed when she had to go to school this morning. Even Mira had fussed when Mrs Arora came to collect her. What was this? Had her children decided to gang up against her?

"What are you doing here?"

Advocate Chowdary was beginning to realise there was something more than just a passing interest between the woman and this French officer. No wonder he had been so agitated the previous morning. Chowdary was not blind. The tension between the two could be cut with a knife. They seemed to have forgotten he was there. This was going to be a very complicated case indeed.

He wiped his forehead with a handkerchief, hastening to explain to the irritated young woman, "I asked Mr Chevalier to come here, Mrs Chari. He has proof of your husband's efforts to terrorise you."

"I'm not pressing charges against Sunil. I just want custody of my children."

"Are you crazy?" Sid pounced on Jasmine. "This is your chance to screw the bastard. He's made you sign those documents that allow him to walk away scot-free."

"This is Mrs Chari's affair, not yours, Officer. Let her decide." Mr Chowdary turned and addressed the woman in a gentle voice, "Do you want to mention the physical, mental, and emotional abuse, Mrs Chari?"

Jasmine shook her head, ignoring Sid, who was glowering at her. "I only want custody of my children. I don't want to make Sunil angry. Let him take the property, money, and whatever my parents gave him. Just file for Reshmi and Mira's custody. That's it."

"Are you sure, Mrs Chari"? Even Advocate Chowdary was doubtful. Like the officer, he, too, felt that Sunil deserved the cell. Those videos made even a hard-hearted man like Chowdary emotional. How could she allow that cruel man to escape?

"Of course, she isn't!" Sid turned to growl at Chowdary. "If that bastard is not backed into the corner, he's *not* going to give her custody of her children. You know it. Why are you not telling her that?"

"Officer Chevalier, I think I made a mistake calling you here. You are right, of course. We have to threaten Sunil with exposure, or he will fight for custody. Would you trust me, please?"

Sid rose from the chair, disappointment eating him as he turned on his heel and walked out. The excitement of meeting Jasmine, talking to her, and constructing a future with her seemed like wishful thinking. He noticed the air of confidence around Jasmine. Unlike before, she didn't tremble when his lips brushed her cheeks. She seemed calm, too calm. He was a fool to have believed he could have this woman. She would always remain a mystery.

He strode to his car, got in, and sat with his hands on the wheel unable to start the engine and drive away. He was tied to Jasmine by some invisible thread. She would never love him with the same intensity that he loved her, but he still wanted to be at her side.

Sid was about to start the car when he saw two tiny figures —one in uniform and the other in a coloured dress—running in his direction. His heart swelled as he saw their excited faces and heard their delighted squeals. Jasmine could probably do without him but not her children. Sid leapt out of his car, feeling energised as he opened his arms.

Reshmi reached him first and had no qualms about climbing him like a tree. Mira was crying as she clung to Sid's leg, and he plucked her from the ground and held them both tightly to him.

"I missed you guys," he said in a shaken voice, his voice trembling with feeling, which triggered their emotions because they wet his shirt with their tears.

"We missed you, Uncle Sid. Don't ever leave us again." Their voices synced.

"I have some explaining to do… Let your mother come… I'll tell you what made me rush off that way. But you must believe me when I say I didn't abandon you. Roy was supposed to arrange your rescue. I had left instructions with him to take over in my absence."

"I know," Reshmi said. "I couldn't imagine you wouldn't. Mom and I spoke to Roy the day we left Residency Towers. It was obvious he didn't want us troubling you."

"Bad Uncle Roy… Bad Uncle Roy," Mira chirped.

From the corner of his eyes, he saw Jasmine exit Chowdary's office and come to a startled halt as she spotted her children with Sid. There was such a sense of betrayal on her face, as if Reshmi and Mira had hurt her by being with him. Sid strode towards Jasmine, carrying Reshmi and Mira in his arms, knowing it was his last chance to woo the woman he loved.

"Would you have a coffee with me, Jess?" His eyes pleaded, and he could see the effort she was making not to be rude in front of the children. They were looking at her with such hopeful expressions that her lips tightened.

"I have to go to work. Mira, Reshmi, get down. You are not children," she told them in stern tones. "Now!"

She was flushed and looked beautiful, her chest heaving in agitation. Sid wanted to lift her, too, and carry the family away.

His mother would be thrilled to have them, he was certain. The fact that they spoke Tamil was a sure plus.

"I'll drop you at work."

"I can take the bus. Put them down."

Sid walked back to the car and dropped the children in the back seat, winking at them. Jasmine was scowling as she was forced to follow them to the car. The look she gave her children told Sid he should not leave their side for any reason. But a closer look at Jasmine, and Sid's heart melted. She was scared. Her hands trembled as she dumped the coins back into the worn-out handbag.

Sid felt an ache in his chest as he thought about the sacrifices she had made to come this far. She was massaging her tired feet after she got into the car, and one shoe turned over. Sid saw the heel was rough with wear and almost worn out. He hoped Jasmine would give him a chance to take care of her. Not that he felt sorry or anything like that. Sid was proud of how Jasmine had handled herself vis-à-vis that madman. He never thought she would leave Sunil's prison without outside help. Jasmine placed her handbag between them, and he thought it rather cute and childlike.

"What did I do to earn your wrath, Jess?" He backed the monster out of the parking lot, throwing her a sideward glance as he swerved with a screech of tyres.

She clenched her hands on her lap, her lips straightening into a thin line. "I came to my senses soon enough."

"Are you saying you don't love me anymore?"

"I never said I loved you. I was grateful to you."

Sid felt as if she had punched him in the gut. Her tone was unemotional, and it was the tone that convinced him she was telling the truth. He thought of all the dreams he had weaved around her, the fights he had with Roy and Becka, and how he had thrown both out of his life without a second thought. Was this a kind of retribution for hurting the people who loved him?

Jasmine hated what she was doing, but she knew she had to do it, or Sid would continue to pursue her out of his obligation to help them. If he had really cared for them, he would have come to their rescue as soon as he learned of their disappearance. She bit her bottom lip as he started to speak. She wanted to hear what he had to say, not that it would make a difference.

"I'm sorry I wasn't there for you and your children, Jess. You might find this hard to believe, but the mother I've been trying to trace for twenty-seven years suddenly called me the day you were abducted."

Jasmine turned and looked at him with a startled gasp. She remembered Reshmi mentioning that Sid had some misfortune in his life and helping them made him feel better. So, that elderly lady was Sid's mother. She was happy for them.

"My mother was the reason behind this quest to save assaulted women. I started Rescue Operations because I couldn't save my mom all those years ago from my father. You know nothing of my past, Jess, but I was given away to a wealthy French family when I was three as Mom suffered physical abuse in the same way you did.

"When I heard her voice that morning, I forgot everything. I rushed to Pondicherry to meet her. My mobile was with you, and the village in which Mom lived didn't have phone booths. When I returned, Roy was tight-lipped, and I thought he was peeved because you rescued yourself before he could intervene. No one mentioned you; it was as if you had disappeared from my life. As a last resort, I called Sunil. He told me you had left with the girls and a money bag. You didn't need anyone, he said. I remember you saying something along those lines: *I need no man to protect me.*

"Until I received my mobile, I had no idea you'd spoken to Roy. But when I came to know what he told you, I fired him on the spot. I sent Becka away, too. I want you, Jess. I love you. I love your children. I want to make you mine."

Jasmine looked out of the window, her eyes misty. She didn't want to live another moment of dependence. She turned her head and said bitterly, "For how long? Until the next crisis?"

She couldn't help it. She understood the part about his mother. But how could she be sure Sid wouldn't leave her again when she needed him?

"I deserved that," he said quietly, bringing his car to a halt on the side of the road. "I love you, Jess. I want to marry you."

"I'm already married. I'm not looking to marry again."

"Then come and live with me and my mother. She's met Reshmi and Mira yesterday." He saw the surprised glance she shot her children and the way they flushed guiltily and realised he had put his foot in his mouth. "She loves them already. She will love you, too."

"And if she doesn't? Would you send me away?"

"No, Jess. I love you. Mom will understand that you come first for me—you and your children."

Jasmine was choked with tears, and it took a while to digest the news. In reality, she was ecstatic. She wanted to leap on Sid and hug him, kiss those sculpted lips that spoke honeyed words. This was what she had been wishing, hoping, and dreaming, and it was finally happening. But she was afraid to believe miracles were possible; after all, experience had taught her that men changed with time.

"At least meet my mom, Jess. Give her a chance to love you."

Reshmi leaned over and tapped Jasmine on the shoulder, and the way she did it made Sid want to laugh. Jasmine turned and glared at her, but Reshmi didn't back down.

"If you don't say yes to Sid, Mom, I will personally strangle you!" she told her mother in all seriousness. "You cry yourself to sleep dreaming of Sid. You wake up thinking of him even if you don't admit it. And you were heartbroken when you saw him with Becka. So now, don't act like you don't care."

Jasmine tried to keep an angry face but found her lips trembling with laughter. Reshmi was too sharp. Jasmine had no idea her daughter had noticed so much. Having said what she had to say, Reshmi sat back and waited.

Mira poked her head and looked her mother in the eye. "Mira loves Uncle Sid," she said, and what's more, the chubby arms went around Sid's neck as she kissed his clean-shaven jaw.

"It looks like I'm outnumbered." Jasmine's voice was somewhat wobbly, the affection her children were showing for Sid making her feel guilty for treating him badly. "Promise you'll never leave us again."

Sid was no proof against Jasmine's tears. With a frustrated oath at the steering wheel that obstructed their embrace, he swiftly lifted her across the seat, pulling her close to his chest.

"I swear, Jess, I'll never leave you or the kids again."

"I can't take a second heartbreak."

"You won't need to." He placed her back on the seat and restarted the ferocious engine.

They reached the security gate, the wheels of Sid's vehicle crunching gravel as he pulled up to the entrance. With a casual wave to Mashraf, the head of security, Sid guided the car through the pathway of towering trees that cast dappled shadows over the path. In response, Mashraf gave a wide, welcoming smile, his happiness palpable at seeing Jasmine and her children safely back. Upon reaching the villa, Sid sprang out of the car, eager to assist Jasmine and lift the girls over the threshold.

"Come! I want you to meet your mother-in-law," he said to Jasmine. "She's gonna love you."

"And if she doesn't?" Jasmine whispered in shaky tones.

"I'll make up for it," he said with a cute grin. "We still have some unfinished business, you know."

Saroja watched from the doorway as her son's car purred to a halt. He was walking happily with two children in his arms. Saroja's smile broadened as she realised they were the same children of the previous day.

"Mira, Reshmi," she addressed them with excitement, unaware their mother was standing beside her Siddhu. Moreover, Saroja still hadn't guessed it was the dreaded Jasmine.

Reshmi and Mira kissed Saroja's cheeks soundly and tugged her towards their mother, standing beside Saroja's son. Saroja's smile wavered as her son's arm wound around the woman's shoulders. She knew who it was now: Jasmine Chari —mother of two, senior to her son, and yet to be divorced. And then she looked at the little girls' faces and found them pleading for approval and then her son's tense face. Slowly and reluctantly, she smiled at Jasmine.

Jasmine was modestly dressed, her beautiful face unmade, her long hair slipping out of the knot as if Siddhu had run his hands through it. She was offering Saroja a timid smile in return. Saroja wanted her son to be happy; he'd had enough unhappiness in his early life. If Jasmine and her children could make her Siddhu happy, then that was all there was. She held her arms open wide.

Jasmine's steps faltered. Her smile widened as she realised that Sid's mother was welcoming her. She ran into Saroja's arms with relief. Reshmi and Mira also embraced their grandmother. Sid watched with a smile as his family entered the villa.

From inside, Sid could hear, "Mira wants chocolate…" Sid grinned as he stepped into the villa and shut the door. There were going to be a lot of 'Mira wants', and he was going to be busy responding to the long list. But for the moment, Sid had wants, too, he thought, as he led Jasmine to his bedroom, saying over his shoulder that he needed classified information about the case.

The look Reshmi gave him said that he could have found

a better excuse to hoodwink them. Sid grinned. He loved these kids, he loved Jasmine, and he had his mother's blessings.

His mobile buzzed. It was Becka. She had received the flowers and thanked him. She had some news that couldn't wait to be delivered. Sunil had done some bogus business deals and evaded taxes. She and Roy were uncovering information that would strengthen their case. By the time they were done with Sunil, he would be willing to settle Jasmine with generous alimony and allow her to keep her children.

Sid closed his eyes and sent up a prayer of thanks. By the sound of it, Roy and Becka were back at work. Everything was settled. Sid and Jasmine had gotten their Passport to Love.

ACKNOWLEDGEMENT

Special thanks to my editor, Vinita Nayar, for her invaluable guidance and expertise in shaping this manuscript into its best form.

ABOUT THE AUTHOR

Cécile Rischmann

Cécile Rischmann is a passionate author and writer who enthusiastically pens short stories, novellas and novels (fiction and non-fiction), has a penchant for poetry and dabbles in scripts and screenplay writing.
She has a double major in French Literature and Human Resource Management, studied Spanish and Italian, went on to do Business English Higher and excelled in Creative Writing.

BOOKS BY THIS AUTHOR

Visa To Paradise

Enticed into accepting an all-expenses-paid exotic vacation, young and rebellious Annette Carmichael is heading to an unknown destination along with her friends for fiesta decadent week of fun and frolic. However, to their shock, they end up at a dilapidated psycho-spiritual center instead!

Dave Carter, an attractive American celibate, with a successful track record of turning rebels around, is asked to take on Annette and her troop. Dave is horrified as his last experience with a woman left him without roof, vocation and reputation. But the center is in financial straits and Annette's parents are willing to invest ...

Annette Carmichael, however, has no intentions of roughing it out in a dilapidated place where even basic amenities are lacking. She's willing to do anything to escape...

But Dave is equally determined to make Annette stay and is ready to use his charm any which way he can to get her on her feet again.

Sweetly intense, brutally honest, and deeply passionate, Visa to Paradise is Cécile Rischmann's second romance novel. In this novel, she wanted to fuse entertainment with value, addictions with new life and new beginnings.

BOOKS BY THIS AUTHOR

The French Encounter

When Jean Leclerc, the young French billionaire decides to construct a glass float in India, he is thinking political and environmental hurdles. So imagine his surprise when he comes face-to-face with a ferocious Bengal Tiger.

Katrina Santiago, a young feisty Indian woman, is saving herself for the one she'll eventually marry. She may work for the French administration, but she does not date Frenchmen. And then she sees JLC in all his splendor. Values and traditions are flying out of the window. She wants him. She wants her one chance at love.

BOOKS BY THIS AUTHOR

A Terrace Affair

Madras in the 80s was an époque of Run-Away-Lover-movies, couples dying for each other, parents playing the villain, and teens falling in love with other cultures and religions. We may not have had landlines, leave alone mobile phones, and those who did have phones used code language and suffered CBI enquiries if the call fell on the wrong ears. But did that stop us from communicating? No, we took to poetry, song and whatnot.

A Terrace Affair is set in this époque. Alia, an Anglo-Indian girl, is faced with the trauma of loving a Hindu NRI boy hailing from a traditional family.

Manoj, a college student, hailing from a chartered accountants' family, is more challenged than fascinated by Alia. Alia's aversion to the caste boy draws him into courting her. With the help of his friend, he plans his strategy and slowly goes for the kill.

A Terrace Affair is a sweet and haunting tale of innocent love, where young lovers waved to each other and passed messages through wrong numbers, where family scrutiny prevented frequent meets and heightened stolen moments of passion.

BOOKS BY THIS AUTHOR

Deception

Adios Amigo

Faced with death knocking at her doors, Anna has to reconsider her forthcoming marriage to the millionaire who has swept her off her feet.

A Passionate Decision

A doubtful heart loses Sushmita her right to love.

BOOKS BY THIS AUTHOR

Julie 1

Julie is only sixteen but so gorgeous that she attracts a smart businessman, Gautam, staying opposite her house. He starts to follow her to school and back, buy her gifts, and charm her with love songs. But, just when Julie starts to develop feelings for him, her parents learn of the romance and decide to put an end to it.

Will Julie defy her folks, or will she submit to family pressure and forget him?

Julie is a sensational short story, inspired by the '70s movie hit JULIE.

Julie 2

Julie's decision to attend Gautam's wedding was an unfortunate one. Perhaps she had secretly hoped that he would tie the thali around her neck, reaffirming their love. Now, all that remained were bittersweet memories from their shared past flooding her heart with tenderness and nostalgia.

As Gautam watched Julie wipe her tears away, his heart felt as if it was violently torn from his chest. If only he had followed his heart, he and Julie could have been united forever, their love enduring through the ages…

BOOKS BY THIS AUTHOR

Wishing For The Moon 1

Ric Coelho—the handsome, green-eyed, twenty-six-year-old CEO of Coelho Estates is about to wed!

Like any wealthy Mangalorean family, his parents choose the beautiful, elite Reshmi, of similar age, community, and status to grace Ric's arm.

Tanya Lobo, a middle-class, thirty-year-old Goan, works as a secretary and lives with her aged, bedridden mother with no money to build her dreams and no father to pay the bills.

And then, one day, Ric knocks on Tanya's door.

Wealth and status lose meaning. Fire and passion ignite. Ric wants the impossible. Tanya wants the moon.

Will their love transcend barriers?

Wishing For The Moon 2

Ric Coelho, the handsome, green-eyed, twenty-six-year-old CEO of Coelho Estates, is about to wed—not the girl he fell in love with, but the girl of his parents' choice!

Tanya Lobo attends his wedding with her aged mother (who hopes Ric will change his mind and marry her daughter instead).

But Tanya knows it is like wishing for the moon...

BOOKS BY THIS AUTHOR

The Donkey

Mocked, Beaten and Condemned...

The Donkey tells the story of a child who endures the physical and mental wrath of her schoolteacher. While Celina's father vows to shoot the witch, and her mother considers buying her a gift beyond their means, Celina refuses to let her teacher destroy the simple pleasures of life. She revels in playing in the rain, swimming in muddy pits, sailing paper boats, and singing on stage.

Two decades later, Celina attends the funeral of her hated teacher. Memories come flooding back, and as she bids farewell to her tormentor, she imparts a few profound thoughts worthy of contemplation.

BOOKS BY THIS AUTHOR

One Night With You

Hailing from a little village in Tuscany, 18-year-old Carina Maraschi hasn't a clue as to how to court a man, so she sings to him like how she'd sing to her cows as she milked them.

CEO of Ricolli Enterprises, Angelo di Ricolli, is in Florence on business. He is intrigued with her voice and somewhat amused that he is flirting with his eyes. When he decides to leave his business card for her, he knows that he is hooked.

One innocent night turns into one swarming with doom, danger and disaster.

Nation-wide romance winning author who has captivated audiences with Jilted, The French Encounter and Somewhere over the Rainbow, strikes again with a romantic thriller, One Night with You, that keeps you on the edge of your seat as her characters love, battle, and betray.

BOOKS BY THIS AUTHOR

Crazy

When Bradley James returns after a five-year absence to resurrect the past, he sees his 'Becka' transformed into the beautiful, sophisticated Rebecca. She hasn't forgotten how he'd abandoned her, and nothing will make her soften towards him.

But when Bradley requests for their favourite song, 'Crazy', Rebecca's eyes start to glisten. In a flash, she's gone back to her teenage years, where she and Bradley had spent an idyllic summer in an abandoned villa. She sees herself strumming her guitar against the backdrop of a storm-tossed ocean while Bradley cooked fish on fire coals.

Will Rebecca let her wistful memories take her down the path of destruction again? Or will she bid Bradley goodbye?

BOOKS BY THIS AUTHOR

P.s. I Love You

In a poignant tale of unexpected connections, Shobita, a young student of psychology, finds herself drawn to the enigmatic Vasudevan in a psychiatric clinic. Amid the challenges of his lockjaw condition, a unique bond forms between them. As they navigate the complexities of pain, loneliness, and the healing power of music, an unforeseen turn of events leaves Shobita grappling with unanswered questions and the haunting melody of what could have been.

BOOKS BY THIS AUTHOR

The Belly Dancer

Deepika travels overseas as one of the finalists from India for an international belly dancing festival in Egypt. One day, while shimmying to the rhythm of the wind and the waves, a striking Egyptian man interrupts her, insisting that Deepika dance for him. One glance into those coal-black eyes and she is breathless... even more so when he introduces himself!

BOOKS BY THIS AUTHOR

Fading Echoes

A resilient and vibrant soul battling pancreatic cancer faces the inevitable. Her indomitable spirit, love for life, and unwavering faith shine through even as her health deteriorates. The narrative explores the protagonist's impactful life, her infectious enthusiasm, and the profound effect she had on others. The tale is a poignant tribute to a sister's enduring strength, joy, and lasting echoes of her presence.

BOOKS BY THIS AUTHOR

Somewhere Over The Rainbow

A bereaved daughter comes to bid farewell to her mother and finds herself swept away in a flood of memories. As she relives her past, she visits moments in her childhood, drawing comfort from happy times and forgiving the not-so-happy ones.'Somewhere over the Rainbow' is a tribute to the author's mother, a bittersweet memoir that's written straight from the heart.

BOOKS BY THIS AUTHOR

One Fine Day

In the heartwarming tale of "One Fine Day: A Tale of Friendship and Learning", follow the charming journey of Sarai, a perpetually sleepy village girl in Chengalpattu, India. When she crosses paths with Theo, the son of a visiting scientist, their unlikely friendship unlocks a world of possibilities.

With humour and heart, this story reveals how kindness, compassion, and the magic of education can transform even the sleepiest of dreams into radiant reality. Join Sarai and Theo on an unforgettable adventure filled with laughter, unexpected alliances, and the enduring power of friendship.

Proof